Thief of Dreams

Thief of Dreams

written by

Todd Strasser

G. P. Putnam's Sons
New York

G. P. Putnam's Sons

a division of Penguin Putnam Books for Young Readers,
345 Hudson Street, New York, NY 10014.
G. P. Putnam's Sons, Reg. U.S. Pat. & Tm. Off.
Published simultaneously in Canada.
Printed in the United States of America.
Designed by Gina DiMassi. Text set in Bookman Light.
Library of Congress Cataloging-in-Publication Data
Strasser, Todd.   Thief of dreams / written by Todd Strasser.
p. cm.   Summary: Thirteen-year-old Martin's parents
are always too busy making money to pay much attention to him,
so he enjoys the attention he gets from his uncle Lawrence,
until he discovers that his uncle has a secret life.
[1. Robbers and outlaws—Fiction. 2. Fathers and sons—Fiction.
3. Family problems—Fiction.] I. Title.   PZ7.S899 Tf 2003
[Fic]—dc21   2002006793
ISBN 0-399-23135-8
1 3 5 7 9 10 8 6 4 2
First Impression

To Geo Goat,
who inspires and teaches.

Table of Contents

Each age is a dream that is dying,
Or one that is coming to birth.
—*Arthur O'Shaughnessy*

Thief of Dreams

The Rich and Very Rich

It's Thanksgiving and your parents have brought you to the club for dinner. A pair of flickering jack-o'-lanterns wear sinister grins outside the front door. Inside, the dark mahogany walls are decorated with dried bunches of red and yellow Indian corn. The sweet scent of roasting chestnuts and yams hangs in the air. On a large round table in the center of the dining room, a wild turkey stands in a bed of orange, red and golden leaves. Dark brown feathers glistening, black beak polished, only its clouded, unmoving eyes give its lifelessness away. At tables all around, martini glasses clink.

What would the Puritans think?

"Something from the bar, Mr. Hunter?" asks Peter, dressed in a black-and-white uniform. Pale pink scalp shows through his thin white hair. His nose is a bright red river system of blood vessels. Loose face flab hangs beneath his pale jaw. He must be 280 years old. You have recently turned thirteen. But here at the club, you call this old geezer Peter and he addresses you as Mr. Hunter.

"Dry martini, straight up, three olives," you reply.

Old white-haired Peter doesn't bat a wrinkled eyelash. He's seen enough wise-guy teenage sons of club members to last a thousand lifetimes.

"Okay, a Coke," you give in.

"Very good." Peter jots it down on his pad. "And for your parents, the regular?"

"You'll have to ask them."

"Very good." Peter trudges away. You slouch deeper into your chair. The dining room glitters. The crystal chandeliers. The plates and glasses and cutlery at your table. The members. Only those who glitter are allowed to join this club.

The Puritans would freak.

Alone, you pass the time by rolling the edge of the tablecloth between your fingers. Two cloths cover this table. A round red one under a square white one with three place settings. Dead center in the gold-rimmed white plates is the club seal—a pair of crossed golf clubs with gold banners flying from their handles. The sparkling long-stemmed wine- and water glasses also have the club seal, as do the many polished silver forks, knives and spoons. Old geezer Peter probably has the seal tattooed on his back. Along with "Property of the Deep Meadow Golf Club."

You loosen your blue-and-red striped tie. Seated all around the dining room are families: men and boys in jackets; women and girls wear dresses and pearls. They dine quietly and speak in low voices. Their glittering silverware clinks softly against the sparkling china.

You, on the other hand, have no one to whisper to. Your father is table-hopping. Stops at each table to shake hands and kiss cheeks. As if he's running for president. Family rules state that Mom must go with him, but she keeps glancing in your direction with a worried look on her face.

Happy Turkey Day, folks. Only, who in this glittering dining room is really giving thanks?

"From now on I want you to stay with us and not go ahead to the table," your father says when he and Mom finally sit down. Your father is wearing a navy blue blazer, a light blue shirt with a white collar and a yellow bow tie. "Did you have to loosen your tie?"

"My collar's too tight."

"I thought Elka just got you that shirt," goes Mom, who is wearing a dark red dress and a string of white pearls.

"It's still too tight."

"Maybe if you watched what you ate," your father mutters.

"I watch everything I eat." To show him, you break off

a piece of bread, paste a large slab of butter to it, study it carefully for several seconds, then shove it in your mouth.

Mom smiles crookedly, but your father is not amused. He gives you the same look old Peter gave you when you asked for the martini.

From the outside, the Deep Meadow Club looks like a huge old stone mansion with endless windows covered by green-and-white striped awnings. Inside, the dark walls are lined with portraits of famous golfers wearing caps, brown knickers and high plaid socks.

People who are very rich join the Deep Meadow Club to play golf with other very rich people. People who are just average rich join the club so they can get to know the very rich people and learn how to be like them. People who are not rich do not join.

One way to tell who is very rich and who is just average rich is that the very rich don't seem to work very hard. On the other hand, the just average rich work very, *very* hard. Your parents are just average rich. You know this because they work all the time.

Who?

"**Y**our mother and I have to go to China for a month," your father announces midway through his pumpkin pie.

Huh? Your parents run a fiber optics consulting firm and they often go away on trips. But never for as long as a month.

"What about Christmas?" you ask.

"We'll be back right before New Year's."

Mom's eyes go soft. "I'm sorry, Martin."

"No, you're not."

Your father's eyes get hard and narrow. "That was uncalled for, Martin, apologize."

"Sorry, Mom." But you're not. Even though you've just finished dinner and a slice of pumpkin pie, you pick up a piece of bread, dip it in your water glass and take a bite. You used to do this when you were little. Your father hated it.

"China is a huge market," he attempts to explain. "Five billion people and they all want telephones. The Chinese government knows fiber optics is the only way to go and they need consultants to show them how to do it. It's a fantastic opportunity. If we don't take it, they'll find someone else."

"It's how we make a living, Martin." Mom always tries to ease the blow. "It's how we afford to live in our house, and pay for this club and take vacations. It's our business."

It's always their business. It's always about making enough money. You've told them a hundred trillion times that you don't care about the house, or this club or the vacations. Dip another piece of bread into the glass. The water turns foggy. Your parents watch uncomfortably.

Your father clears his throat. "Uncle Lawrence will stay with you while we're away."

"Who?"

"My brother," he says.

"Never heard of him."

"Remember Lake Tahoe?" Mom asks.

"Oh, *that* uncle."

She arches an eyebrow. "The only uncle you've got."

It's just a sliver of a memory. Three or four years ago. Your parents rented a house at Lake Tahoe for Christmas week. One afternoon you and Uncle Lawrence sat in the hot tub while it snowed. Clumpy white snowflakes fell into the steamy water and disappeared. Just like parents.

Eavesdropping

ou and your parents moved to a new house over the summer. This one is fully networked. The phones are hooked into the computers with E-mail, intercom, a family message center. The ultimate in intrafamily communication. You could probably go weeks without any real face time with your parents. Also, you can eavesdrop on them in just about any room in the house.

"This is a terrible idea," Mom tells your father. They don't know you're listening on the intercom. "You've hardly spoken to Lawrence since Lake Tahoe."

"It'll be fine," your father replies. "He'll only be here for a month."

"We don't know where he's been or what he's been doing."

"He does the same old thing. Moves from place to place and job to job. He's just one of those people who can't settle down and stick to anything."

"And this is the kind of person you want taking care of Martin?"

"He's harmless. And he's my brother, for Pete's sake."

"Your brother who you rarely talk to, who dropped out of high school, who disappears for months at a time."

"Everything will be okay," replies your father. "Elka will be here, too."

"Is that supposed to make me feel better?" Mom asks sharply.

"Let's face reality." Your father's voice drops to a more serious level, almost a snarl. "The last place I want to go for Christmas is China. But we need this work. Business has been slow, and with this new house our expenses are higher than ever. If we don't take this job, I can't promise we'll make it through next spring."

"So Lawrence moves into our house for a month," Mom summarizes. "Are you going to tell him the code for the alarm system?"

"Of course."

"What if he tells someone?"

"He wouldn't."

Silence.

"Okay, if it'll make you feel better," your father promises, "I'll change the code as soon as we get back from China. That way, even if he does tell someone, it won't matter."

More silence, then from Mom: "All right. But this is the last time I leave Martin for this long."

The World's Most Beautiful Babe Psychologist

Of all
The people
In the world
The last one
I want to be
Is me.

T hank you, Martin." Dr. Rodriguez folds the small piece of blue paper. "Can I keep this?"

"Only if you laugh."

Dr. Rodriguez, the World's Most Beautiful Babe Psychologist, blinks her dark, almond-shaped eyes. "Why?"

"Ever since you stopped wearing that ring you've been sad." A thin band of skin on her left ring finger is a lighter color than the skin around it. Until two weeks ago she'd worn a small diamond ring on that finger. Sometimes while you talk she touches the place where the ring used to be.

Rubbing her hands together, Dr. Rodriguez says, "You're very observant, Martin."

"What happened?"

"That's personal. It's nice of you to ask, but we're here to focus on you, not on me." She recrosses her legs and tugs the hem of her purple skirt over her knees. Always wears skirts that are just long enough to tug over her knees when she's sitting. Probably tells the tailor she wants them that length so there'll be no peeking.

She holds up the folded blue paper with your poem. "Did you really want me to laugh?"

You shrug. You're big on shrugging. A major-league shrugger. You take shrugging practice. It's probably one of the few things you do well.

"I don't think you did," Dr. Rodriguez says. She has long brown hair that is so dark, it sometimes looks black. It's shiny in a way that makes you suspect she puts stuff in it that keeps it straight. Her olive skin is smooth. Everything about her is gentle and delicate. Once a week you're supposed to tell her what's bothering you. It's her job to listen so that your parents can stay focused on work.

Dr. Rodriguez leans forward and rests her elbows on her knees. "Your parents are going to China for a month?"

"Uncle Lawrence is gonna stay with me."

She wrinkles her forehead. "I don't . . . recall you mentioning him before."

"That's 'cause I never have."

"Who is he?"

"My father's brother."

"Have you ever met him?"

"Once."

She sits back and crosses her arms. Her eyebrows are squeezed in tight. "Where does he live?"

"Don't know."

"Is he married?"

"Not a clue."

Dr. Rodriguez displays a major frown. It is not her style to comment on how your parents raise you, but you know she thinks they're doing one seriously lousy job.

Uncle Lawrence

He stands in the front hall wearing a long black leather coat. A coat your father would never dream of wearing. He is shorter than your father, and thinner, and looks younger. His short blond hair doesn't have any of your father's gray. His eyes are bluer, without bags under them. His face doesn't have those deep worry lines. Doesn't wear glasses like your father. Wears a light blue plaid shirt with snaps instead of buttons, blue jeans and scuffed brown cowboy boots. When it comes to people over the age of eighteen, you don't generally think about looks, but Uncle Lawrence is one handsome dude.

Mom seems tense and nervous. Her hands won't stay still. Her eyes dart at your uncle as if searching for clues to a mystery. "I'll let you two get to know each other," she says, but stays in the front hall straightening the flowers. You and Uncle Lawrence watch until she looks up and realizes you're waiting for her to do what she said she'd do. "All right, if you need anything, just give a yell. I'll be in the den. Martin, you can show Uncle Lawrence the house."

She leaves. Your uncle glances at the gold-framed paintings, the floor-to-ceiling mirror, the big vase of flowers, the white marble floor.

"Guess I'll get my stuff," he says.

"I'll help," you offer.

"Nah, that's okay."

He goes back out the front door. You follow. He may not want your help, but he didn't say you couldn't watch. His cowboy boots crunch on the white pebbles that cover the driveway. A plain dark red sedan is parked by the curb. It's a sunny late November day and the car's finish sparkles as if it's just been washed. Uncle Lawrence opens the trunk.

"A rental?"

He turns and focuses on you. "How'd you know?"

"It's like the ones my parents rent when we go on trips. Besides, the key."

The key, which is still in the trunk, has a bright yellow Hertz fob.

"Very observant," Uncle Lawrence says, which is kind of weird because it's what Dr. Rodriguez said, too. He reaches into the trunk and pulls out a small carry-on-size black suitcase.

"Should I get the other stuff?" you ask.

"Okay, sure."

In the backseat are two plastic milk crates. One's filled with CDs, some books and magazines on astronomy. The other crate has a radio alarm clock, a portable CD player and a pair of binoculars.

"You like astronomy?" Lugging one of the crates, you follow Uncle Lawrence into the house.

"Sure do."

"Bird-watcher?"

"Huh?" He looks back over his shoulder, spots the binoculars. "Oh, yeah."

"There's one around here I've never seen before. White belly, the rest dark gray. About the size of a sparrow."

"Sounds interesting."

"Know what it is?"

"I'll have to check on it."

This new house is vast and spread out, mostly on one floor except the part where the bedrooms are, which is the second floor. That part of the house is like a house in itself. Your parents have a big bedroom suite with an attached bathroom and a walk-in closet. Your bedroom's up there, too, along with the den where your father watches sports on the weekends. On the first floor are two guest bedrooms, a small gym with the indoor/outdoor pool behind it and a game room with darts, Foosball and air hockey.

Uncle Lawrence goes into the guest bedroom with the

sliding door next to the indoor/outdoor pool. Inside he starts to unpack the black carry-on. You leave the milk crate and go back out to the car. The trunk's still open and inside is a long black cloth bag and a medium-size case made of shiny silver metal. Photographers carry cameras and lenses in cases like this. Grab the handle and try to lift it out of the trunk, but it's heavy and you don't want to risk dropping it. Bring in the other milk crate instead.

In the guest bedroom, Uncle Lawrence is putting his clothes in the dresser drawers.

"I tried to bring in that metal suitcase, but it's too heavy."

"I'll take care of it," he replies.

"What about the long black bag?"

"Telescope. It can stay in the car."

That means there's nothing left for you to bring in. Lean in the doorway. "You must have a lot of cameras in that thing."

"What thing?" he asks.

"The camera case."

Your uncle raises his head and thinks for a second. "Oh. Right."

"What for?" you ask.

"Taking pictures, what else?" He goes back to un-packing.

"Where's the rest of your stuff?"

He looks up again. "What do you mean?"

"I thought you were staying for a month. This is hardly anything." Gesture at the two milk crates and the now empty carry-on bag.

"Right. The rest is back home."

"Where's that?"

Uncle Lawrence gives you a look. "You ask a lot of questions."

"Sorry, it's none of my business, right?"

He takes the astronomy books out of the milk crate. You figure it's time to go, and start backing out of the door.

"Hey," he says, "go ahead and ask all the questions you want."

"Okay." But you leave anyway.

Night Vision

Uncle Lawrence has gone out somewhere. Stop outside his room and peek in. On the bed is a red, white and blue Priority Mail carton about the size of a toaster oven. It's open and you can see white Styrofoam peanuts sticking out. No one's around. Do you go into the room and take a closer look? You're not supposed to. Your parents like you best when you do what you're supposed to do. But your parents are going to China. For the next month this uncle you hardly know will be in charge of you. Maybe what's in the box will give you a clue about him.

Tiptoe through the doorway and look inside the box. In a clear plastic bag is a gray scope that looks like half of a pair of binoculars. According to the booklet, this is a generation-three night-vision scope. Feel your eyes widen. What's he need *that* for?

A car pulls up in front of the house. It's around dinnertime, so it can't be your parents. Most nights they don't come back from work until much later.

Bail out of Uncle Lawrence's room and head for the kitchen. Elka, the latest blond nanny from Denmark, has just taken two chicken pot pies out of the microwave. She places one on the kitchen table for you. She'll eat hers at the counter, chewing slowly and gazing into nothingness.

Hear the front door open and close, then footsteps in the hall. A comet enters the kitchen, slicing through the galaxy of silence. Uncle Lawrence in a gray sports jacket and black slacks. The collar of his white shirt is open, no tie. His slacks have a nice crease. Elka stares at him.

Your uncle takes in the scene—you eating at the kitchen table, she eating at the counter. His forehead bunches.

"Smells good," he says.

Elka doesn't seem to know how to deal with this compliment. As if Uncle Lawrence is speaking in a strange language.

"Hungry?" you ask.

"Thanks, but I just came in to get something. I'm going back out."

"Where?"

He gives you a slightly amused look, as if you've said something funny.

"Oh, right," you realize. "It's not polite to pry."

"No, it's okay," he says. "I'm just not used to it, that's all."

"How come?"

The corners of his lips lift a fraction closer to smile territory. "You mean it or just joking around?"

"Both."

"Well . . ." Slides his hands into his pockets. "I guess most people just aren't that curious. Let me ask *you* a question. How come you're so curious?"

"Just the way I am. You can tell me if I'm being nosy."

"No, it's good to be curious. How else are you going to learn anything?"

"Okay, so where *are* you going?" you ask, now that you have his permission.

"Thought I'd check out Mars," he answers. "M19 and M62 should be pretty easy to find. And if I get lucky, I might even get a glimpse of M6 and M7. See ya." He gives Elka a small wave, then leaves the kitchen. Listen to the front door open and close. Outside a car engine coughs and revs.

You and Elka exchange a glance. The comet may have gone, but its tail of shimmering crystals lingers.

"What is M19?" she asks.

"I think it's like a galaxy. In space."

"Oh." She thinks for a second. "He's nice." She's talking about Uncle Lawrence, not M19.

"Yeah."

"He's really your father's brother?"

"Hard to believe, huh?"

Elka lets her jaw fall in mock surprise. She blushes bright pink, then presses her finger to her lips.

The Long Dark Night of Eighth Grade

T o avoid the cafeteria at lunch, you eat in the library and surf the Net. The library, aka media center, is the primary school portal into cyberspace. Clusters of computers on round white tables. Socially you might as well be in Siberia. Or Cyberia in this case. It's lonely here on the frozen tundra of the social outcast. You sit alone, pretending you're in an igloo, waiting for the long dark night of eighth grade to end.

Here's how it works when you wear glasses, are new at school and are in serious need of a major growth spurt:

Go into homeroom. The kids look at you. Their eyes don't say hello. Their eyes say good-bye.

Go into class. The kids who aren't in your homeroom look at you. Their eyes say good-bye.

Go to gym. They don't even look at you.

Except for the tall, gangly kid with loose black hair

and a dirty shadow over his upper lip. Wears red plaid hunting shirts, baggy olive military pants and large, clunky, unlaced boots often crusty with dried light brown mud. Fingernails always have dirt under them. Walks alone through the halls. Possibly a few French fries short of a Happy Meal. So, of course, he's the only one who acts friendly.

His name is Wendell, and he also spends lunchtime at a computer in Cyberia. As you pass his igloo, you notice he's looking at a photo of a night-vision scope that looks exactly like the one you saw in Uncle Lawrence's room.

Sensing your interest, Wendell twists around. "Cool, huh?"

His pungent breath reminds you of older dogs. Or, possibly, the garbage dump on a hot summer day. You fight the urge to gag. In English you recently learned the meaning of the word *dilemma: a situation involving a choice between two equally undesirable alternatives.*

Here is your dilemma. Either act like you don't care about the scope and leave, thus missing the information you want. Or get the information, but only by being friendly to Wendell, and suffering with his horrible dog breath.

Tough choice, but as usual, curiosity wins. You stay with your hand politely covering your nose.

"This is a generation-three scope," Wendell explains,

tapping the computer screen with his dirty fingernail. "Way clearer than generation two."

"It really works?" you ask.

Wendell gives you the what-rock-did-you-just-crawl-out-from look. "Night vision? Of course it works. The Army uses it. Cops, too. Don't you watch TV?"

Don't admit that you always suspected it was some pretend thing, like time travel and DARE. Instead, ask, "You wouldn't use it to look at stars, would you?"

He shakes his head. "You'd use a telescope."

"Right. Thanks." You have to get away before his breath makes you barf. If you ever talk to Wendell again, you better bring a gas mask.

Brainiac Sherpas

Sunday morning. Except for the chirp of a bird and the hum of the pool filter, it's quiet. Back in September distant sounds sometimes came from beyond the trees. Laughter, splashing in pools and the *thock* of tennis balls. By the middle of October it was quieter. By late November, almost silent. Your neighbors' yards are hidden behind trees and tall hedges. Their houses are tucked away at the ends of long, curving, tree-lined driveways. Maybe they all flew south for the winter.

In the kitchen, your father reads the *Wall Street Journal.* The front of his gray sweatshirt is dark with sweat. He's wearing blue gym shorts, so you know he's been working out in the home gym.

"How come you don't read the local paper?" you ask.

"Nothing important in it," he replies. "You want to know what's going on in the world of business and politics, you read this. You want to know about the new

Home Depot, you read the local paper." Your father closes the *Wall Street Journal*. "Which reminds me, we have to stop at the new Home Depot and get a Christmas tree stand."

"If you never read the local paper, how do you know there is a new Home Depot?"

Your father scowls. He misses the irony in this.

Every now and then, when he can take time off from his busy schedule of work, exercise and golf, your father attempts to do something "fatherly" with you. Today he's decided that you and he will get the Christmas tree together.

"What's the point?" you ask as the two of you walk toward the three-car garage. "You won't even be here for Christmas."

"We always have a tree." Your father stops in front of the garage. All three electric doors are open. Inside is his shiny new silver Mercedes, Mom's older, dull blue BMW station wagon, and the car they let Elka use—a scuffed and dented old red Volvo.

He decides to take Mom's BMW. Every time you get into a car with him, he asks the same question: "How are things at school?"

"Okay."

"Your grades?"

"Fine." School is easy for you. You get B's when you don't study and A's when you do. As long as you get good grades, it takes a lot of pressure off your parents. "I got moved up to a higher math class. They don't even teach it at the middle school, so I go over to the high school four times a week. Most of the kids are sophomores and juniors."

Get a curt nod from your father. As if being moved up in math was expected all along. The problem is, it's not really so good. Hiking over to the high school four times a week just makes you seem weirder to your classmates. Only three eighth graders make the trip. You, Wendell and a tall blond girl you don't know. Each day the blond girl leaves school first and walks about fifty feet ahead of Wendell. You follow about fifty feet behind him. With your heavy backpacks, the three of you trudge up the hill to the high school like brainiac Sherpas. Meanwhile, all the kids on that side of the middle school gawk out the classroom windows at you.

"Friends?" says your father.

"Sorry?" You'd drifted off, lost in the woes of the brainiac Sherpas.

"Have you made any friends?"

"I'm doing okay."

"Good." Now that he's asked about school and friends, he can turn on the radio. An oldies rock station comes on. Mom listens to it when she's alone in the car. Your father switches to AM and finds the twenty-four-hour all-news channel.

• • •

Travel down a rutted dirt road lined with bare gray trees, then pull into a muddy parking lot. Light brown water quickly fills the tire tracks. Your father has come prepared, wearing black rubber boots. You're wearing shoes.

"Sorry, I forgot my boots," you apologize.

"So I see." Eyebrows severe. He's ticked.

"Want to skip it?"

"No, we're here." He reaches for the door handle. "Let's go."

Outside, your shoes sink into the mud. Icy cold water seeps into your socks. In the chilly, damp air your breath comes out in white mist. The sky above is a slab of gray. Follow your father to a clearing where a blue plastic jug filled with free hot chocolate sits on a folding table. Fill a paper cup and pluck a couple of chocolate chip cookies from the pile on a blue plate.

Nearby, two men dressed in work boots, jeans, plaid shirts and down vests stand around the yellow tube that bags trees in a cocoon of white plastic mesh for the trip home. Not far from them is the squat yellow machine that shakes the dead needles out of the branches. The guy next to it looks gangly familiar.

It's Wendell, wearing a sweat-stained green John Deere cap, a heavy blue plaid shirt with holes at the elbows, jeans with black grease stains and mud-caked boots. Brainiac Sherpa farm boy.

Your father pulls a bright red metal cart with bicycle-size wheels down the dirt path toward the field where the trees grow. You follow, eating chocolate chip cookies and sipping hot chocolate.

"Know that boy?" he asks in a low voice.

"He goes to my school."

"Don't hang around with him, do you?"

"No."

The field is divided into different types of trees. Silvery blue-green spruce, greener Scotch pine and Douglas fir. In your family it is generally agreed that the blue spruce is the best-looking tree. But beauty has its costs.

"Can't we get a Douglas fir this year? The blue spruce needles hurt."

"Because you don't wear gloves."

"It's hard to hang Christmas ornaments with gloves on."

"I do it."

Trek down rows of bluish green spruces and stop next to a nice-looking tree. "How about this one?" you ask.

"Not bad," your father replies, then moves on. No point in telling him that icy cold water has completely drenched your shoes, and your frozen feet are slipping around inside squishy slimy socks.

"They used to make medicine from pine needles," you proclaim.

"Oh?" Your father considers a blue spruce that looks just like all the other blue spruces you've passed.

"They made tea from the needles. Pine needle tea."

"What do you think of this one?" He crosses his arms and studies the tree as if it is a painting by Picasso. Feet numb, you've started to shiver. Your father glances in your direction when he hears your teeth chattering. But real men have always faced obstacles in the pursuit of the perfect Christmas tree, and you shall be no exception. He reaches into the cart and hands you the saw.

"Why me?"

"You're thirteen, Martin."

The saw is a red metal tube bent like a small bow. A gnarly-looking blade spans one end of the tube to the other. The ground around the tree is covered with scattered hay. Kneel and feel the cold wetness seep through your pants to your knees. The fresh scent of pine lingers in the needles just inches from your nose. Part the lowest branches and peek in at the rough brown trunk, which is about the same width as a baseball bat. Reach in with the saw. To get the blade on the trunk, you must press in against the sharp, pointy pine needles. They scrape against your glasses and nick your forehead and cheeks.

Push and pull with the saw. But kneeling into the tree, you can't get much pull and even less push. To get closer, you lie down on the wet ground and slide under the lowest branches. Cold ground water invades your clothes and shocks your skin. The shivers that run down your arms make your hands tremble. But cutting the tree is strangely rewarding. The blade rips through the soft wood, and the air under the branches grows sweet with the scent of freshly cut pine.

The blade shears clear through. Your father angles the tree down onto the cart. You get up. The wet side of your body is chilled, your pants and jacket are darkly splotched with water, dirt and loose strands of hay. But you feel an unexpected surge of pride.

Martin Hunter, slayer of pine trees!

You clench your fist and puff out your chest. Maybe when you grow up you'll be a lumberjack.

Then your father points at the tree's trunk. "See how you cut it on a slant? Next time try to make it straight."

Feel your shoulders sag. *Martin Hunter, never does anything right.*

Double Tap

Since your parents will soon leave for China, they arrange for you to spend more time alone with Uncle Lawrence.

"Hey!" His voice makes you jump. You've been playing the computer with earphones on and didn't hear him open the door. Slide the earphones down around your neck.

"Didn't mean to yell." He leans in the doorway, wearing the blue checked shirt, jeans and beat-up cowboy boots. "I knocked but you didn't answer."

"It's cool."

"So what's up?" he asks.

"Nothing."

"Whatcha doing?"

"Playing Grand Theft Auto."

"Can I see?"

You shrug. He comes closer and watches over your

shoulder while you explain the game: "You earn money by stealing cars and shooting people. A few steps removed from Go Fish. Even a grown-up can understand."

Uncle Lawrence feeds you the typical "uh-huh"s and "no kidding"s.

Pause the game and look over your shoulder at him. "You don't have to pretend."

He frowns. "What makes you think I'm pretending?"

Not sure what to say, you turn back to the game and continue playing.

"You're pretty good with this thing," he says over your shoulder.

"The computer? Everyone's good at this."

"Not me."

Pause the game again; turn to look at him. "For real?"

"Never learned."

Who doesn't know how to use a computer? Even your grandparents, who are like, dead, send E-mail and book vacation cruises on the Internet.

"You don't really have to *learn*."

Uncle Lawrence chuckles. "Right. You're born knowing."

Almost answer yes. Then realize that you did learn, only it was back when you were still in diapers or something. Meanwhile, Uncle Lawrence moves around your room, checking out the junk on your shelves.

"What about college?" you ask.

"Didn't go."

Right. Mom said he didn't even finish high school. Way hard to believe. You thought everyone went to college. It's almost like required. Check that. Definitely required in the Hunter family.

On your windowsill is a bowl of water filled with green, blue and white sea glass. When the sunlight hits it, cool aqua reflections get projected on the far wall above your bed.

"You had a turtle?" Uncle Lawrence asks.

"No."

"Just glass?"

"Yup."

He studies it a moment more. "Gotcha. It is what it is." Slides his hands into his pockets. "What do you do besides play computer games?"

"Listen to music."

"Which you do while you play computer. What else? How about sports?"

"I'm captain of the basketball team. Can't you tell?"

He scowls, then gets it, and smirks. "Come on."

"I'm not much of an athlete."

"Your dad's a pretty serious golfer. Ever play with him?"

"A couple of times. He says I slice too much. He wants me to practice my drives before he takes me again."

"Want to go to the driving range?"

"Now? It's cold."

"Bet we can find one that has heat."

Shake your head. "It's boring."

Uncle Lawrence smiles.

"What's so funny?" you ask.

"You remind me of me. I hated practicing, too. Your dad would practice all the time. Go to the driving range and hit buckets of balls. Or shoot foul shots for hours in the driveway. I'd watch TV."

"What about video games?"

"Them, too. Only they were nothing like today."

"Want to go?" you ask.

"Where?"

"The arcade."

"Sure, why not?"

At the arcade, get in the token line behind a tall red-headed kid wearing a black T-shirt and baggy green pants. Wendell style.

"You don't have to stay," you tell Uncle Lawrence.

Inside it's dark, noisy, filled with kids and flashing screens. A few grown-ups stand around waiting while little kids play.

"You don't want me hanging around?" Uncle Lawrence asks.

"I just don't want you to feel like you have to."

"Wait a minute," he goes. "Didn't *you* ask *me* to come?"

"Yeah, but . . . Okay, fine, whatever."

Double Tap is your favorite game. Big screen and two

plastic pistols on cables. Pick up the blue pistol. Uncle Lawrence takes the red one. Get into your basic cop-show two-handed stance. Aim down the barrel and blow the bad guys away. Next to you, Uncle Lawrence is the one who's getting blown away. He keeps forgetting to reload, and goes through three times as many quarters as you. By the time you both finish the first level you've got ten times more kills than him.

He rubs his gun hand. "Thought you said you weren't good at anything."

Feel a little ping of pride. Like what you felt a few days ago when you killed the Christmas tree. But not really.

"Not at anything important."

"What's important?"

"I don't know. School. Sports. Stuff that makes you popular."

"I bet you do well in school."

"How would you know?"

"Just strike me as the type. Besides, I know my brother. He wouldn't accept bad grades. You'd have been shipped off to boarding school by now."

It's weird when someone you don't know seems to know you. Or did your parents secretly prep him? *Here's the file on Martin. Read it, memorize it and destroy it.*

"What about you?" you ask.

Uncle Lawrence raises one shoulder and lets it drop. "Got thrown out of every boarding school they sent me to."

"Then what?"

"They quit sending me."

Study him, recalling the conversation you overheard between Mom and your father. *High school dropout.* It sounds so extreme. Everyone finishes high school, don't they? "You can do that? Just stop going?"

"Sure. You don't want to go to school, who's going to make you?"

The Dinnertime Thief

Nine-thirty at night. Your parents have just gotten home from work. The red intercom light on your phone blinks. Mom asks: "Martin? Would you join us for dinner?"

You answer: "Already ate."

"We'd like your company anyway."

It's like attendance.

The kitchen is all white. The walls, the stove, the biggest refrigerator you've ever seen in a house, the dishwasher, the floor, the table and chairs. White on white on white. The white microwave hums. Your father is standing by the white kitchen counter in his suspenders and tie. The sleeves of his white shirt are rolled up. He sifts through the mail and glowers at the microwave. Annoyed that it won't cook faster.

Mom's sitting at the white kitchen table, checking E-mail on her cell phone (silver, not white) and doodling on the back of an envelope. She looks up at you, smiles, keeps scribbling. Her doodles are all lines and arrows and little junctions with letters labeling them. You do stick figures; she does ether networks.

The microwave bings. Your father takes out two steaming plates of roast chicken, mashed potatoes and string beans. Brings them over to the kitchen table and sits down. Pokes the mashed potatoes with his fork. "From a box."

Mom takes a nibble. "Not bad."

"I thought we told her to make them from real potatoes," your father grumbles.

Mom spears a green bean. "It's not that important."

"Let's order Chinese tomorrow," you suggest eagerly. "To get you ready for the trip."

Your father clears his throat. "We're leaving in the morning."

"But you can have Chinese if you like," adds Mom.

"Great." You can't get enough of General Tso's chicken.

Your father taps his finger on a yellow flyer from the town baseball league. "Want to sign up for Babe Ruth in the spring?"

"Could you coach?"

He knits his thick, dark eyebrows. "I can't get home early enough."

"How about you, Mom?"

She straightens up. "Me?"

"Moms coach baseball."

"I don't know anything about the game."

Your father steals home plate. "Let's talk about what happens while we're away."

"No parties." Mom winks.

"We expect the security system to be on at all times," adds your father.

"Even when I'm home?" you ask.

"*Especially* when you're home."

"You worried about me being kidnapped?"

"No," answers your father. "But this is a big house. You could be in your room watching TV while someone was in another part of the house."

That's more like it. For a moment it almost appeared that he was concerned about you.

"You probably don't remember what happened in Lake Tahoe," Mom says. "All those burglaries Christmas week."

"That's right," your father recalls. "During dinner parties. People would be downstairs entertaining while the burglar came in an upstairs window."

"They called him the Dinnertime Thief," Mom adds.

Uncle Lawrence comes into the kitchen, wearing the gray sports jacket and black slacks from the other night. Mom forces a stiff smile onto her face. "Hello, Lawrence."

"Going out?" asks your father, although the answer looks pretty obvious to you.

"Thought I would."

"Had dinner?" you ask. "Want to eat with us?"

"We don't really have anything," your father blurts. "I mean, nothing that's ready."

Weird thing to say, given the size of the refrigerator and the fact that it's always full. Also, this is your parents' last evening at home and it might be nice if you all ate together. Now that you think of it, the four of you haven't eaten together once.

"I'm sure I could whip up something," Mom quickly injects.

"It's okay."

"No, really. Let's see what's in the fridge." Mom starts to get up.

"Actually," Uncle Lawrence begins, then pauses as if he's not sure what to say. "I'm meeting someone."

You'd be willing to bet your Barry Bonds autographed baseball that he just made that up. Mom freezes and seems uncertain. "Where?"

"Le Bicyclette."

"Very nice," goes your father. "Make sure you have the crème brûlée."

Mom sits down. Lots of awkward eye motion follows. As if no one's sure what to do, or say, or believe.

Uncle Lawrence checks his watch. "Well, see you in the morning."

He's just starting to turn away when your father asks, "You've got a tie, don't you?"

Your uncle stops. "No."

"You'll need one."

"No. Just a jacket."

"And a tie," your father insists. "Absolutely."

"I don't think so," Uncle Lawrence says.

Your father crosses his arms, buries his chin in his chest, and gives Lawrence a five-star how-dare-you-question-my-authority look. Like what generals in movies and police captains on TV do when some dimwit with the intelligence of a tree stump doubts them. Or what some older brothers might do when they think their younger brother is a complete idiot.

You'd think Uncle Lawrence would laugh it off, or maybe go get a tie just to be safe. Instead he squints back at your father with a look that tells him to go spend eternity in a very, very hot place where the landlord has horns and a tail.

And then he's gone.

"Did you have to do that?" Mom asks your father after the front door slams shut.

"He never listens," your father mumbles, and cuts into his chicken.

Mom purses her lips and gives you a concerned look. She's leaving for China in the morning, and you can tell she's unhappy. Uncle Lawrence wouldn't be her first choice of baby-sitter. Or second.

Dead Giveaway

A rare sunny December day. Blue sky. Drag a ladder onto the basketball court beside the garage. The court is a square patch of asphalt measuring twenty-five feet by twenty-five feet. Painted a shade of green that matches the grass. From a distance it looks like a black pole and glass backboard have been placed in the middle of the lawn.

When you were younger, your father would sometimes play b-ball with you in the driveway of your old house. You'd do one-on-one for ten or fifteen minutes but then he always had something else to do. He'd tell you to stay and practice. Dribble a ball with each hand at the same time (he got you two balls so you could do this). Practice bounce passes against the garage wall. Practice foul shots, layups, jumpers, fadeaways. Practice, practice, practice.

"You'll never be the best if you don't practice," he'd say.

"Maybe I don't want to be the best," you'd reply.

"Of course you do. Everyone wants to be the best."

You just wanted to have fun. Playing b-ball with your father was fun. Practicing wasn't.

Now, on this warm December day, the low harsh winter sunlight glares off the glass backboard and makes you squint. Prop the ladder against the pole. On TV you once saw this big buff basketball dude slam-dunk so hard that the entire glass backboard turned white and shattered. Ten zillion glimmering shards of glass rained down and splashed on the basketball court.

Hear the crunch of pebbles under tires. Mom's blue BMW station wagon comes up the driveway. It's Uncle Lawrence. No sense paying for a rental all month. He'll be using Mom's car until she comes back.

"Setting up for a slam dunk?" he asks.

"How'd you guess?"

"Ladder's a dead giveaway."

"Hold this?" Hand him the basketball, then start up the ladder. "You need a tie last night?"

"Decided to go somewhere else," he answers.

The top of the ladder feels awful high. You're a bit queasy up there, but determined to complete your mission. Real Christmas tree killers can slam-dunk. "Okay, ready."

Uncle Lawrence keeps the ball tucked under his arm. "Pretty long way down."

"I can do it."

"Didn't say you couldn't."

"So give me the ball."

"Look, Martin, don't put me in a position where I have to call your parents on their first day in China and tell them I watched you break your leg."

"I won't break my leg."

"Promise?"

You can't promise.

"Then come down, okay?"

Darn him. "But just so you know, I would have done it."

"I believe you."

Soon as you're off the ladder, he bounce-passes the ball to you and heads for the house.

Put the ladder back in the garage. Go into the kitchen to get some water. Your parents have recently installed an expensive water cooler after seeing one in a neighbor's house. As a major act of rebellion you still drink from the tap.

Finish the glass, look up at the kitchen clock. Almost time to go see Dr. Rodriguez. Outside, the garage door is open and the Volvo is gone. Strange. Elka's never forgotten to take you before.

How will you get to Dr. Rodriguez's? You could ask Uncle Lawrence, but you're not sure you want to. It's that guy thing about seeing shrinks. Don't go around broad-casting it, right? Announcing to the world that Martin Hunter sees a shrink because . . . Well, just because . . .

But you're supposed to go, and while you don't always do the little things you're supposed to do, you generally do the big things. A moment later you're standing outside Uncle Lawrence's door with your hand raised, poised to knock. From inside comes an odd, squishy, almost tearing sound, followed every few seconds by a metallic click. You know you've heard a sound like it before, but you can't remember where.

Knock.

"Just a minute." The clicking sound stops. Now you hear a rustle. *Something being shoved under the bed?*

The door opens. Uncle Lawrence is wearing gray slacks and a blue shirt, like he's getting ready to go out. "What's up?"

"Elka's not here and I have to go somewhere."

"No problem. That's what I'm here for."

Night Work

A black wooden coatrack stands in the waiting room, along with some black chairs and a low black table with magazines. The office door opens. At the sight of Uncle Lawrence, Dr. Rodriguez stiffens. Your uncle extends his hand. "I'm Lawrence Hunter, Martin's uncle."

"Very nice to meet you." Dr. Rodriguez shakes his hand, then shifts her eyes to you. "Come in, Martin."

Follow her down a short hallway with a painting of red flowers on the wall. Ahead is the door to Dr. Rodriguez's office. On the floor a small round sound machine makes a loud whirring hum so someone using the bathroom can't hear what patients are talking about.

In the office, Dr. Rodriguez settles into her usual seat and pulls the hem of her black skirt over her knees. You pick up a yellow Nerf ball and start thinking about a shot that involves banking the ball off the bookcase, then off the wall and into the miniature plastic hoop on the inside of the office door.

"Did your parents give you Christmas presents before they left?" she asks.

"A new CD burner and a Swiss Army knife." You found them under the tree this very morning, just after your parents left for the airport in a big black car.

"Is that what you wanted?"

"The CD burner, definitely. The Swiss Army knife is the gift for the kid who already has everything." Take the shot. The ball banks off the bookcase, hits the wall, then nicks the edge of the miniature plastic hoop before dropping to the floor. A near miss.

"Have you ever thought about going out for basketball?" Dr. Rodriguez asks.

"No way."

"Why not?"

"I'd never make it. Fifty kids went out for the team this year."

"You could try."

"Know where Nerf comes from?" you ask.

"Sorry?"

"Nerf, like in Nerf ball." Hold the spongy yellow ball out toward her and squeeze it until your fingertips practically meet. "No one knows. Even the guy who invented it doesn't know. He just decided to call it Nerf."

"We were talking about basketball."

"You were, not me. Want to know something else cool? The guy who invented the Nerf ball also invented Twister. With the plastic mat and the polka dots? You spin the spinner and have to put your hands and feet on the dots."

"Oh, yes. The one where people have to climb over each other."

"Right. The first game ever to use human beings as game pieces. Is that amazing or what?"

"I'm sorry, Martin. Is what amazing?"

"That the guy who invented the Nerf ball also invented Twister. I mean, think of the millions . . . no, *billions* of people who have played with Nerf balls, and then think of the billions of people who've played Twister, and they never knew they were invented by the same guy."

Dr. Rodriguez thinks about that. "What about after-school intramurals?"

"Where kids choose up sides? I'm always the last to get picked."

"You could prove them wrong."

Line up the next shot and let it fly. The Nerf ball hits the bookcase at the wrong angle and drops straight to the floor.

"See?" This proves you stink. Flop down on the couch and check your watch. Wish you could get out of there.

Dr. Rodriguez studies you quietly. "You were having fun shooting baskets. I asked you about playing basketball, and now you're slumped on the couch counting the seconds until the session ends."

Shrug.

"Could you give me more than a shrug?"

"Could *you* give *me* a break?"

"You're angry."

"No duh."

"Why?" she asks.

"Know what's funny about glass?"

"I'm sorry?"

"Glass. What's funny about it."

"No . . ."

"Sometimes it's more beautiful when it's broken than when it's whole."

Dr. Rodriguez does her quiet thing. Like she's trying to understand the deep dark meaning of this. Right now your parents are probably somewhere in the air over the Novosibirskiye Islands in the East Siberian Sea. The fastest route to China being more or less over the North Pole. They are going there to advise the Chinese government on fiber optics—thin threads of glass that carry electrons a thousand times faster than old-fashioned copper wires. They don't realize that families are sometimes made of glass, too. And that family glass is not shatterproof.

Minutes pass in silence. Sometimes Dr. Rodriguez lets this happen. Finally, she changes subjects. "Is Mr. Hunter taking care of you now?"

"No. Well, I guess in a way. Elka wasn't around today."

"How do you feel about him bringing you here?"

"It's okay. I mean, it's not like it's a big secret or anything. I don't think it's going to change his opinion of me."

"What does he think of you?"

"That I'm an okay kid and as long as I do what I'm supposed to do we should get along."

"Do you think you could do more than just get along?"

Funny how sometimes she can read your mind. But that's probably why she's a shrink.

"Maybe."

"Would you like that?"

"I guess. He stinks at Double Tap."

She raises her chin, interested. "He's played with you? That's very nice of him."

"He didn't do it because he's nice. I mean, he is nice, but I think he liked it."

"Do you think you'll go to the mall with him after our session today?"

"No, he's dressed like he's going out."

"Where does he go?"

"He's into astronomy. Or maybe he's going on a date. I don't know."

"Is it possible that he goes to work at night?"

"Maybe." You hadn't thought of that.

Newly Discovered Alien Species

P ass stores on the way home with shiny red and green Merry Christmas lettering strung in the windows. Sidewalks lined with bare gray trees. Houses draped with too many blinking, glittering lights. Uncle Lawrence drives without speaking. No radio. He seems used to silence.

"Dr. Rodriguez asked what you do at night."

"Mostly look at the sky. Sometimes go to a movie. Or dinner."

"Do you work?"

"I'm between projects right now."

"What kind of projects?"

"Different things."

Wanting to ask what kind of things, but not wanting to seem too nosy, you ride in silence, and enter Deep Meadow Estates, the neighborhood where you live. Here and there a glimpse of a stately house appears through the dark bare trees. Instead of gaudy strings of Christmas glitter, tasteful candle-shaped lights glow in the windows.

"You haven't asked me what kind of things," Uncle Lawrence finally says.

"Figured it was none of my business."

"I've worked for pool maintenance companies. Been a locksmith, a chauffeur, even crewed on a yacht in the Mediterranean."

"Don't you get lonely moving around so much?"

"Sometimes."

It's dinnertime when you get home. The house is filled with the aroma of grilled lamb.

"Hope you're hungry!" Elka calls from the kitchen. Has she ever sounded that cheerful before? Not in a long time. But it's understandable. The nanny agencies tell the nannies that they're going to be part of this cool American family and travel and have a fabulous time. Then the nannies get here and find out most parents don't want them to be part of the family. They just want them to keep the house neat and run errands (you qualify as an errand). And it's not like nannies can just hop a plane back to Denmark and return to milking cows or whatever. They're stuck here. Like minimum-security prison. As a result, nannies often develop Major Attitude, a contagious disease like mono or head lice that prevents them from being cheerful.

So what's with Elka wearing a blue-checked apron and pulling a rack of lamb out of the oven?

"Smells great," says Uncle Lawrence.

Her face lights up, cheeks turning red at the points of her mouth. Instead of the usual ponytail, her blond hair is brushed out over her shoulders and shimmers under the kitchen lights. She points a fork at the two place settings at the kitchen table. "Sit. It's ready."

You and Uncle Lawrence sit. Elka bustles around, serving and pouring like Little Miss Homemaker. Mixed into the aroma of roast lamb is the faintest scent of perfume.

"Where were you this afternoon?" you ask.

"The car," Elka answers. "I got a flat tire. I tried to call you, but the cell phone wouldn't work. You made it okay?"

"Dude over here brought me."

Elka gives Uncle Lawrence an Olympic-size smile. "Thank you." Picking up a long knife, she starts to slice the lamb. Delicious-smelling steam rises from each incision. You begin to eat. Elka takes her usual place at the kitchen counter.

"Aren't you going to sit with us?" Uncle Lawrence asks.

Elka brightens even more, and you realize that this is exactly what she was hoping for. "Are you sure?"

Uncle Lawrence turns to you. "Are we sure?"

"Sure we're sure."

Elka picks up her plate and joins you at the table.

"This is really good," Uncle Lawrence says, then shoots a look in your direction.

"Delicious," you say on cue.

"Thank you!" Elka is smiling to the point of bursting. Who would have thought a simple compliment would make her so happy? Then again, you can't actually remember your father doing anything except grumbling about her.

"So how do you like it here?" Uncle Lawrence asks Elka.

Good-bye smile. Elka avoids your gaze. She might have a lot to say if you weren't there.

"I didn't mean *here* in this house," Uncle Lawrence quickly adds. "I meant, here in this country."

That's better. Elka launches into the basic America's-so-big-and-everything's-so-fast routine. Face flushed, she is more animated, more talkative than you've ever seen her.

"You're a pretty girl," Uncle Lawrence says when she's finished. "Have you met any guys here?"

Elka blushes and shakes her head. Does this have something to do with the makeup and brushed-out hair? Doubtful. Elka's nineteen. Uncle Lawrence has to be more than twice that.

"What does your father do?" Uncle Lawrence asks.

"He's a lawyer," she answers. So much for milking cows.

"And your mom?"

"A *psykiater,*" Elka says in Danish, then laughs self-consciously because you don't have a clue what she means. She points at her head. "A doctor of the head."

"A neurosurgeon?" you ask.

Elka frowns. Now it's her turn to not understand. To show her what you mean, you pick up your knife and fork and cut into a lamb chop. "Like a surgeon."

Uncle Lawrence bursts into laughter.

"No!" Elka cries. "Not this." She mimics cutting. "This." She mimics writing notes on a pad.

"Oh, a *psychiatrist,*" you realize.

Still chuckling, Uncle Lawrence dabs a tear from his eye.

"What's so funny?" you ask.

"A neurosurgeon?" He imitates you sawing into your lamb chop with your knife. "Pass the steak sauce, Nurse Betty." Next he picks up a bone. "Hey, look what I found in this guy's brain, Doc."

"Yuckity-yuck-yuck," you mutter playfully.

It feels as if dinner ends pretty quickly. So you're slightly amazed to discover you were eating and talking for almost two hours.

Uncle Lawrence checks his watch. "Gotta go." Dabs his lips with the napkin and stands up. "Thanks for dinner, Elka. It was real tasty."

He mimics cutting with a knife and fork again. "See you later, Doc." And leaves. The kitchen grows quiet. Just

Elka and you and a bunch of dirty dishes. A strange moment, like right after the movie ends and you suddenly realize you're back in the real world.

Elka gazes at the door Uncle Lawrence just went through. "He sees someone?"

"All I know is he looks at the stars."

She cups her hands against the window and presses her face close. "It's cloudy."

"Guess he's not looking at stars."

Her gaze drifts down to the dirty plates on the kitchen table, then over at the greasy pots and gravy-stained cutting board by the sink. She sighs grimly. Rolls up her sleeves to do battle.

"Want some help?" you ask.

"Oh, no." She looks *shocked* that you offered.

Normally you'd go back to your room. Tonight you join her at the sink. "I'll rinse, you load."

Elka's eyes widen. As if perhaps you're a newly discovered alien species. Maybe you are.

Wet Suit

The dishes are done. Elka's gone to watch TV. You pass Uncle Lawrence's room. Stop by the door. Where *does* he go at night? The answer could be on the other side of this door. Try the knob. Locked. Start to turn away, then remember. There's a small hole in the middle of the knob.

Are you really going to break into your uncle's room? You shouldn't. But who is this grown-up who actually seems to like playing video games? Gets dressed up at night and goes out you don't know where?

The doorknob turns when you stick a screwdriver in the hole. Flick on the light. Bed's made. No photos of loved ones on the night table. No favorite print on the wall. No effort to make the place homey. He could just as easily be staying in a motel. Something tells you the day your parents return from China, he's out of here.

Step farther into the room and look around. Heart

thudding. Hands trembling. Now that you're in here, you shouldn't be so nervous. You'll hear the car if Uncle Lawrence comes back.

No sign of the night-vision scope.

Drop down to your knees and look under the bed.

Nothing.

No, wait, what's this? A thin scrap of rubbery black material about an eighth of an inch thick. You've never looked at a wet suit closely, but you'd bet this is the stuff it's made of. Recall those squishy sounds, followed by that metallic click—scissors cutting through this stuff.

"Martin?" Elka's standing in the doorway. "What are you doing?"

"Nothing." Spring to your feet. Slide the scrap of black material into your pocket. Your heart accelerates to near-bursting speed.

"You shouldn't be in here," she scolds.

Running on autopilot, you hurry past her out into the hall and up the stairs to your room. Sit on the bed and take out that black scrap. Study it closely. Why would anyone cut up a wet suit?

Losers Club

L ooked like you got a good tree," says Wendell. It's gym and you're too busy trying to play Ultimate Frisbee to discuss Christmas trees. This could be the break you've been waiting for. Your chance to show everyone that you are not a half bad Frisbee player, and that in spite of your slight chubbiness, glasses and lack of a visible growth spurt, you are a seriously cool dude. Ultimate Frisbee will be your ticket out of lunchtime in Cyberia, and into a seat in the cafeteria.

You sincerely believe that this is not a severe mutation of reality. Which is why you are jumping around waving your arms, yelling "Over here!" again and again.

You know they see you.

You know they hear you.

But they never throw the Frisbee to you.

Your throat begins to burn from yelling.

Finally you get a stitch on the right side of your stomach. Feels like someone has clamped a pliers around your liver and started twisting. Stabbing pain doubles you over. Your face feels hot, your forehead damp.

Wendell stands beside you, arms crossed. His Bart Simpson T-shirt has a big hole in the armpit and his shorts are too tight and too short. "Join the club," he says.

The losers club.

"You work at that farm?" Hands on knees, you gasp for breath and wait for the stitch to pass.

"Work and live. It's my dad's. You just move here?"

"Yeah. Over on Phillips Hollow Road."

"Never heard of it," Wendell says.

"It's up around the Deep Meadow Golf Club."

Wendell gives you a toothy grin. "I got a hole in one once."

"No way."

"Way, dude. Over at Buzzy's Mini-golf on Route Twelve."

Doc

Want to hit the mall?" It's Saturday afternoon. Uncle Lawrence stands in the doorway of your room.

"You don't have to baby-sit me."

"Who said I was baby-sitting you?" His eyes shift left, then right. Never enters a room without scanning it first. Making sure no one's hiding behind the bed or in the closet. His eyes fix on the Swiss Army knife on your desk.

"Where'd you get this?"

"Early Christmas present."

He bends back the screwdriver, can opener and half a dozen other features whose functions you're not certain of. This goes on for a few seconds longer than you'd expect.

"You've seen those before, right?" you ask.

"Sure. Just haven't looked at one closely in a long

time." Strange thing about Uncle Lawrence. Like not going to college and not knowing how to use a computer. Almost as if he's been in a time capsule. Apart from the rest of society for the last twenty years. "Last one I saw had two blades, a can opener and a corkscrew. You realize how many tools this would replace?"

"That's the whole idea."

"Right, I'm just saying . . ." He catches himself, puts the knife back on the desk. "So what do you say, Doc?"

He has called you Doc ever since the night you used your knife and fork to demonstrate neurosurgery. First time you've ever had a nickname. You like it. Cool kids get nicknames.

"I'm okay here, really."

"Scared I'll beat you in Double Tap?"

"Not a prayer."

"Prove it," he dares you.

That's it, you're going to the mall.

Later, at the arcade, your hand has started to cramp from gripping the plastic pistol so tightly.

"Hungry?" Uncle Lawrence asks.

"Always," you answer.

"The food court special?"

"Cool."

You sit at a white metal table that's bolted to the floor. The chairs are bolted, too. Chow down on a plate of General Tso's chicken. Uncle Lawrence eats his beef and broccoli with chopsticks.

"That was fun," he says, of Double Tap.

"You're getting better."

"Toward the end there I almost had you."

"No way."

"First two levels."

"They make it easy at first to suck you in, then it gets hard. Strictly a learning curve thing. Meanwhile they rake in the quarters."

A woman strolls into the food court. You see her, look away, then back again. "Dr. Rodriguez?"

She turns. "Martin?" She glances quickly at your uncle.

"You remember my uncle."

"Yes, of course."

He stands and offers his hand. "Hello again."

Dr. Rodriguez's lips part as if she's about to say something. For a moment no words come out. Then: "Yes, hello. Nice to see you."

"Want to join us?" you ask.

"Oh, no, that's sweet, Martin, but I was just leaving."

"No, you weren't. You were strolling in like you had all the time in the world."

Her olive skin reddens. You're not sure you've ever seen her blush before. You feel bad because you didn't mean to embarrass her.

"Sorry," you sputter.

"It's all right." Dr. Rodriguez brushes a few strands of dark hair out of her face. "You're right. I shouldn't have said that."

"I'm sure you have dinner plans," Uncle Lawrence says. "But maybe you'd like to join us for a cup of coffee?"

"Well . . ." Dr. Rodriguez touches her ring finger. The thin band of skin is still slightly lighter than the rest of her hand. But not as obvious as it was a few weeks ago.

"There's probably some kind of rule against psychologists hanging out with their patients," you tell Uncle Lawrence. "But we swear we won't tell."

Your uncle raises his right hand. "Scout's honor."

Knowing she's beaten, Dr. Rodriguez smiles. "Oh, okay."

"So let's see." Uncle Lawrence rubs his chin as if thinking. "You look like the espresso type. Or maybe a cappuccino."

"I can get it," Dr. Rodriguez protests.

"Absolutely not," Uncle Lawrence insists. "You're our guest. Besides, it's proper food court manners."

"All right. If you insist, a mocha Frappuccino, please."

This is your basic coffee-flavored chocolate milk shake. A lot of kids in your grade drink them. Uncle Lawrence lets his jaw drop in a teasing way. "You're kidding."

"They're my secret vice," Dr. Rodriguez admits.

"Ah, the secret vices of lady psychologists!" Uncle Lawrence jests. "Be right back."

He goes off. Hasn't seen a Swiss Army knife in years, but knows what a mocha Frappuccino is. Go figure. Dr. Rodriguez sits down across from you. She seems uncomfortable.

"Just get here?" you ask.

"How do you know?"

"You're not carrying any bags."

"I can window-shop for hours," she says.

"Can't make up your mind, huh?"

She laughs. "Would you please stop analyzing me, Martin?"

It's weird to see her outside the office. She's nervous. Her movements are stiff and her eyes dart around quickly. Is she worried someone will see her talking to a patient? Who would know?

Uncle Lawrence comes back with the mocha Frappuccino. "Here you go." Mr. Cool slides into his seat and relaxes. "You think they bolt these tables and chairs down to keep people from stealing them?"

"Or so they won't be moved where the mall owners don't want them," Dr. Rodriguez guesses.

"Imagine if one disappeared." Uncle Lawrence looks under the table. "It wouldn't be that hard. All you'd need is a wrench."

"And a very big shopping bag to hide it in," Dr. Rodriguez adds.

"Ah, true," says Uncle Lawrence. "Unless you came disguised."

Dr. Rodriguez grins playfully. "As?"

"Let's see." Uncle Lawrence leans forward and props his chin on his fist. "Acme Mall Table Repair."

Dr. Rodriguez and your uncle smile at each other. She's more relaxed now, sipping her Frappuccino and sitting easier in her bolted-down chair. It's the warming effect your uncle has on people.

"I'm gonna check out some posters," you announce. Before they can argue, you're out of your seat and crossing the broad corridor. Past the fountain filled with pennies, and into the poster store. The air has a sweet incense scent. The bored-looking girl behind the cash register has dyed spiky red hair, a black leather choker with silver studs and a gold stud under her lower lip. You don't really want to be there, but you don't want to leave either.

Back in the food court, Uncle Lawrence and Dr. Rodriguez are still talking. You're too far away to hear what they're saying, but Dr. Rodriguez's eyes have a sparkle. If this were the movies, they'd make a good couple. She being so pretty and he being so handsome. Serious magnetic rays are drawing them toward each other. But this isn't about physics. Looks more like biology.

Air Hockey

You okay, Doc?" Uncle Lawrence asks on the way back from the mall.

"Sure." Through the car's windows you gaze out at plastic Santas on their sleds, and Nativity scenes. *'Tis the season . . . for your parents to be in China.*

"Can I ask you something personal?" he asks.

"I'm an open book."

"Your parents don't spend much time with you, do they?"

"It's not like I'm a little kid."

"Did they spend much time with you when you *were* a little kid?"

"They had a lot to do. Build the business and stuff."

"And your mom was okay with that?"

"They're a team. My father finds the clients who need the work, and he makes the deals with them. Mom's the one who really knows about fiber optics. She even writes articles for technical magazines. She's sort of famous in that field."

"I didn't know that."

"She's pretty quiet about it."

"So my brother can't really do business without her?"

"Well, I guess." You never thought of it that way.

That night Lawrence goes out to look at stars or night birds or whatever he does. Elka goes to a nanny friend's. Pop the lock and slip into your uncle's room again. You're getting good at this. A regular cat burglar. Look around. Still can't figure him out. He's like the back page of *Mad* magazine. Appears to be one thing, but fold along the dotted lines and he's something else altogether.

So what is he?

You spot the long leather coat hanging on a hook behind the door. Now that you think of it, you haven't seen him wear that coat since he got here. Touch the sleeve. The leather is smooth and pliable. Its rawhide scent fills your nose. Pockets beckon to be searched. Dare you, Mr. Cat Burglar? Go on, no one's going to know. Slide your hand into one pocket, then the other. Find a gum wrapper, a short stubby pencil, a red M&M. Real exciting, huh? No, but your heart's beating hard anyway. Now try an inside pocket, and there's something in it.

A slim black wallet. Seems a bit odd that Uncle Lawrence would leave it behind. No money inside. Only a few plastic cards. One is an Arizona driver's license with his picture on it. The next is a membership card for the Tucson Health and Sports Club. It also has his photo.

Wait a minute. It's your uncle's photo, but the name on the card is Stuart Barnes. That's the name on the driver's license, too. The last card is a Visa from the National Bank of Tucson. Photo of Uncle Lawrence; name—Stuart Barnes.

The phone on Uncle Lawrence's night table rings. You jump about five feet. Wallet and cards fall to the floor. You're shaking like the dead-needle machine at Wendell's farm. The phone keeps ringing while you catch your breath and try to calm down. Then you answer.

"How's it going?" your father asks, long-distance from China. His voice so clear, he could be across town.

"Okay." Cradle the phone against your shoulder. Pick up the cards and slide them back into the wallet.

"Things okay with Elka?" Mom asks.

"Yeah."

"Everything okay with Lawrence?" asks your father.

"Yeah." Put the wallet back in the inside coat pocket.

"Things okay at school?" Mom asks.

"Yeah."

"Have you got our phone messages?" asks your father.

Put down the phone and go into the kitchen and read him the phone messages.

"We miss you," Mom says when you're finished.

"I miss you, too," you reply automatically.

"Well . . ." The tone of your father's voice means he wants to get off. Long-distance calls from China must be expensive.

"Remember that time we went to Lake Tahoe?" you ask. "Did Uncle Lawrence ski with us?"

"He doesn't ski," your father answers.

"Why, Martin, does he want to take you skiing?" Mom asks.

"Maybe," you answer. "So what did he do all day?"

"I don't remember," your father replies.

"Why do you ask?" asks Mom.

"Just wondering."

"Well, Martin, it's good to hear your voice," says your father.

"Did he go bird-watching?" you ask.

"When?" your parents ask at the same time.

"At Lake Tahoe."

"I don't think so," Mom replies. "Why, Martin?"

"Did he go out at night and look at stars?"

In the silence between you and your parents you detect faint hints of other distant conversations on other distant phone lines.

"It was years ago, Martin," goes your father. "Who remembers?"

"I think he went to the casinos," goes your mother. "Why are you asking?"

"Just wondering."

"I really think it's time to get off," your father says.

But Mom isn't ready. "These are unusual things to wonder about."

Just then you hear a car outside.

"Gotta go. Talk to you soon." You hang up.

Back in your room. Sit on your bed and stare at the bowl of sea glass. Bad people use fake IDs. Like the terrorists who destroyed the World Trade Center. Why would Uncle Lawrence have them? He couldn't be a bad person, could he?

Rap! Rap! The knocks on your door make you jump. Your uncle eases it open. His eyebrows in a deep V. Eyes piercing. Like he's got X-ray vision. "Any idea why the phone in my room's off the hook?"

Slowly shake your head. Good thing he can't know how hard your heart is pounding. He picks up the Swiss Army knife. Snaps out the blade, and studies it. Your lungs begin to hurt. Need to take a breath, but feel like you've forgotten how.

Snap! Uncle Lawrence closes the knife. Looking grim and serious, he tilts his head toward the door. "Is it my imagination, or is that an air hockey game in the game room?"

Huh? You're caught totally off guard. "It's your imagination."

He smiles. "Want to play?"

Feel light-headed. Try to make sense of this. "Uh, sure. Meet you in there in a second, okay?"

"Right." Your uncle leaves, pulling the door closed behind him.

Flop back on the bed. Gaze at the ceiling. Let out a long sigh and try to breathe. That was *way* too close.

Your father got the air hockey game a few years ago. You played him a couple of times, but he always beat you and you quickly got bored with it. When you arrive in the game room, Uncle Lawrence is ready to play.

"Know what this thing's called?" You hold up the plastic thingie you hit the puck with.

"No." Uncle Lawrence puts the black plastic puck in play. It flies back and forth across the table, angling off the sides, clattering loudly.

"Neither does anyone else."

Clack! Clack! The puck is bullet fast. Your eyes can barely follow it. "It's either called a goalie, a striker or a paddle. The funny thing is, no one can agree."

"What do you want to call it?"

"I like 'the plastic thingie.' "

"Fair enough."

Clack! Clack!

"You're not holding it right, you know."

Uncle Lawrence looks down. "I'm not?"

"You don't wrap your hand around the top like it's a

gear shift. You're supposed to put the tips of your fingers in that groove."

The puck slides to a stop in a corner. You show him the proper way to hold the plastic thingie.

"You're just a fountain of information, Doc," he says.

Start playing again. *Clack! Clack!* Uncle Lawrence is okay at this game. Nothing great. You outscore him two goals to one. Pull off your sweatshirt and wipe the perspiration from your forehead. Your uncle yanks a blue bandanna from his back pocket and does like-wise.

Play another game, peel another layer. Both of you down to T-shirts now. Yours is white with a tur-quoise parrotfish on the front. Uncle Lawrence's is your basic gray athletic T. On the front, in arcing black letters, is:

ARIZONA WILDCATS

Clack! The puck flies past you. Uncle Lawrence scores. You hardly notice. That's a T-shirt from *Arizona* State University. Worn by Uncle Lawrence, who never went to college. But Stuart Barnes is from Tucson. And Tucson is in Arizona.

"What happened?" Uncle Lawrence asks.

"Huh?"

"You stopped playing."

"Oh, sorry." Pull out the puck and start to play again. *Clack! Clack!* The aroma of sweat fills the room. Under-arm odor is a new development in your life. The sweat tickles as it runs down the inside of your arm. This can only be a positive sign. Where there is dampness, hair may soon sprout.

Uncle Lawrence smacks in another goal and finally wins a game.

"About time," you tease.

He wipes his forehead with the blue bandanna. "Want to get something to drink?"

Elka's in the kitchen. "Exercising?" she asks when she sees the two of you all sweaty and red-glowy-faced like a couple of X-treme jocks in a Mountain Dew commercial.

"Just creaming Martin," Uncle Lawrence replies while he fills a glass from the tap.

"Creaming?" Elka repeats. Her English is good, but not *that* good.

"Beating the pants off him."

Elka looks at your waist as if half expecting to see you without pants.

"He's trying to say he beat me in air hockey," you explain.

"Hockey?" Elka glances at the kitchen window. It's dark outside. "Where?"

"Come on, we'll show you."

Back in the game room you play Elka in air hockey while Uncle Lawrence coaches her. Being new to the game, her movements are awkward and slow. Sometimes she misses the puck entirely.

"Keep your eye on it," Uncle Lawrence urges.

Elka's forehead is dotted with sweat. She hunches over the table, gripping her plastic thingie tightly. But the puck is often past her before she can react.

"You have to keep your eye on it," Uncle Lawrence tells her again. She purses her lips and studies him for a second, then turns back to the game. *Clack!* Without even meaning to, you bank in a slow-moving shot and win ten-zip.

Elka balls her hands into frustrated fists. "Oh, Martin!"

"You really have to keep your eye on the puck," Uncle Lawrence repeats.

Elka spins around and glares at him, then picks up the puck . . . *and holds it against her eye.* "Like this?"

You all laugh. With glistening red faces, everyone heads back to the kitchen for more water. The three of you stand beside the sink, gulping down glass after glass.

"That was fun," Elka exclaims.

"If I lived in this house, I'd play all the time," Uncle Lawrence muses.

"I have news for you," you tell him. "You *do* live in this house."

Your uncle's lips shift into neutral. He even looks a little sad, as if he wishes he really did live here, wishes he could stay and play games with you forever.

Cyberia

Lunch in Cyberia. Wendell hovers beside your igloo. He's wearing baggy olive green pants and a black T-shirt that says in crooked white letters *We're all here because we're not all there.*

"You like crossword puzzles?" he asks.

You're doing the crossword in the local newspaper. Wendell is just trying to make conversation. Out here in Cyberia, you could even say he's trying to break the ice. Only his hot-summer-day-garbage-dump breath forces you to put your hand over your nose as if pretending to scratch it.

Wendell points. "Thirty-six across is *aces.*"

The clue for thirty-six across is a four-letter word for "pitching stars."

"You read it upside down?" you ask.

"Yeah, no big deal."

So the kid is smart. You knew that, since he and you are two of the three brainiac Sherpas who climb the hill to the high school four days a week for math.

Wendell looks around to make sure no one is watching, then sits down in your igloo. From his pocket he pulls a small black device the size of a phone pager. He presses a button and it plays back the conversation you just had: *"You like crossword puzzles? Thirty-six across is aces. You read it upside down? Yeah, no big deal."*

No pauses between the voices. If no one talks, the recorder stops recording. You take the device from Wendell.

"Voice-activated digital recorder. Cool, huh?"

"Where'd you get it?" you ask.

"Office Depot," he answers. "But you can get them just about anywhere."

That afternoon you visit Office Depot. Back home, you slip into Uncle Lawrence's room and place your new digital voice recorder on the windowsill behind the curtain. On the floor are some shopping bags from the mall. Can't hurt to look, can it? In one of the bags is a large white box held closed by a thick green-and-red ribbon with a bow. There's a card taped to the ribbon. Inside the card, written in some of the worst penmanship you've ever seen, is this:

MY DEAREST,

THOUGH OUR TIME TOGETHER HAS BEEN SHORT, I
FEEL AS IF I'VE KNOWN YOU ALL MY LIFE. THE HOURS
WHEN I'M NOT WITH YOU ARE MEANINGLESS. THE
MINUTES WE'RE TOGETHER MEAN EVERYTHING. MERRY
CHRISTMAS.

TRULY YOURS,
LAWRENCE

Way to go, Uncle Lawrence! Looks like he's got a
honey. Maybe life isn't so lonely after all. Check the next
shopping bag, expecting another Christmas present, but
inside is a black nylon athletic bag with a blue-and-
yellow manufacturer's tag still attached. Unzip the bag.
Inside it are three more black athletic bags, each one
with a manufacturer's tag. Bags inside bags. Fake IDs.
What's this all about?

Merry Christmas

hristmas Day. The house feels quieter than normal. Elka gives you a CD called *Dark Side of the Moon* by this 1970s band Pink Floyd. You give her a pair of turquoise earrings. Uncle Lawrence is gone all day and doesn't show up until dinner. Elka's cooked a delicious turkey, but your uncle is quiet and distant. You and Elka give each other puzzled looks, but neither of you knows what to say. Out of nowhere, your uncle raises his head as if he just remembered. "Hey, Merry Christmas."

"Merry Christmas," you and Elka reply.

"I hate to say it, but I forgot to get you guys presents."

"It's okay," Elka and you both blurt.

Uncle Lawrence grins. "What do you think I am? A chump?"

He leaves the kitchen, then returns with two boxes wrapped in bright green and red gift paper. "Merry Christmas, guys."

Elka gets a pink sweater with little red heart-shaped buttons down the front. "Oh, thank you so much!" She gives him a hug. Your uncle actually blushes.

You get Nike's latest top-of-the-line basketball shoe.

"Wasn't sure of your size," Uncle Lawrence begins to apologize, "but they said you could exchange them."

Press one of the shoes against the bottom of your foot. It's too small, but you don't want to make him feel bad. "Looks pretty close."

You give him a whole roll of arcade tokens. Elka's present is a puffy white terry-cloth bathrobe with the initials *LH* in blue.

Uncle Lawrence blinks. No, he *can't* be blinking back tears. They're just Christmas presents. "Thanks, guys, really. It means a lot to me. More than you can imagine." As if to steady himself, he places his hands flat on the table. "Elka, that was a great meal. Doc, what do you say we do the dishes?"

"You don't have to," Elka protests.

Uncle Lawrence is already on his feet, rolling up his sleeves. Follow his lead and roll up yours. The idea is to let Elka relax, but she bustles behind you, clearing dishes from the table and straightening up. This is seriously different from every other nanny who's ever lived with your family. Not that any of them ever had the choice of not doing the dinner dishes, but if they had, they would have bailed out pronto.

The dishes are done. Now comes a moment when no

one seems sure what to do. You get an idea. "Hey! Who wants to play air hockey?"

Uncle Lawrence lowers his head as he dries his hands on a dish towel. "Sorry, Doc, I have to go."

Feel your face fall. He was gone all day.

"Come on," Elka says. "I'll play you."

Double Gravity

T he day after Christmas. The loudest sounds are the hum of the pool filter and the faint gurgle of water in the pipes when someone turns on a faucet. The whole world is away skiing or sunning. Even Wendell has gone to visit relatives upstate.

Morning blurs into afternoon. A plain purple-colored sedan is parked in the driveway. The trunk is open and Uncle Lawrence is leaning into it. You go out. The air is cool and crisp. The weak winter sun plays hide-and-seek with gray-white clouds.

"Hi," you say. Uncle Lawrence abruptly straightens as if caught by surprise. *Thunk!* He bangs his head hard on the trunk latch.

"Darn!" Holding his head, he staggers back. You're about to start apologizing when you glance into the trunk. That silver case is open. The one Uncle Lawrence said contained camera equipment.

Only it doesn't. Inside is a sheet of dark gray foam with dozens of shapes cut into it. Each shape contains a tool. Some look like things a dentist would use, with pencil-thin handles and skinny, pointed ends. There are wire cutters, small screwdrivers and wrenches. A set of cigar-size flashlights. A small Polaroid camera. A box of black latex gloves. Lying beside the silver case is a neatly folded black jumpsuit with a thick black zipper.

Finally, there's a small cordless drill with a double layer of black rubber sewn tightly around it. It's wet suit rubber like the scrap you found in Uncle Lawrence's room. To deaden the vibrations? No, more likely to muffle the sound.

Bam! The trunk comes down hard. The air rushes against your face. Uncle Lawrence has one hand on the trunk, the other on the spot where he banged his head.

"Gee, I'm really sorry," you gasp. "Is it bad?"

"It's okay," he half groans.

"Want me to get some ice? Or aspirin or something?"

"Just give me a second." He takes his hand from his head and looks, as if expecting to find blood.

"I'm really sorry, really."

"I know." He says this as if he means it, not in a sarcastic way. Way different from how your father would react. He'd be screaming at you.

"Can I do anything?" you ask.

"No, Doc. Just go inside, okay?"

Cross the driveway. Glance back as Uncle Lawrence gets into the purple car and drives away.

You don't have to ask why he has another rental car. Your parents will be home in a few days. He'll be leaving soon.

It's dark. In your room, thin shafts of silvery moonlight squeeze around the edges of the blinds. You lie in bed wondering why you woke. Then you hear the faintest sound of crunching gravel.

Slip out of bed and peek through the blinds. A dark figure in the moonlight lifts a black athletic bag out of a dark car. The bag sags on both ends and pulls the handles tight. The figure crosses the thin patch of grass to the garage and goes in through the side door.

The garage remains dark. Your eyes start to feel heavy. Sleep pulls you down like double gravity. Just when you're about to crawl back into bed, the figure comes out of the garage. No bag. He walks across the lawn and disappears around the side of the house. You hear a door by the pool slowly slide open, then close. He's come in.

The door to Uncle Lawrence's room stays closed all the next day. You're on the computer when the phone rings. It's probably your parents.

"Martin?" It's a woman, and she sounds oddly familiar.

Then it hits you. "Dr. Rodriguez?"

"Uh, yes, I'm, er, calling to check on your next appointment. Is Thursday at five still okay?"

"Sure, why wouldn't it be?"

"I'm, umm, just checking. A lot of my patients are away for the holidays and I want to make sure I know who's coming and who's not."

"I'll be there." It's not like you have anything better to do.

"And . . . will your uncle be driving you?"

Huh? She's never asked who'd drive you before.

As if she senses your curiosity, she adds, "I'm just asking because I found the information he was looking for."

"What information?" you ask, before you have time to realize it's none of your business.

"About family dynamics and sibling rivalry," she explains. "I could give it to him now . . . if he's there."

"He hasn't come out of his room yet. He might still be sleeping."

This time the silence comes from Dr. Rodriguez's end of the conversation. You can imagine what she's thinking: It's four in the afternoon and your uncle's still asleep?

"When he gets up, would you let him know I called?"

"Sure."

"All right. Then I'll see you on Thursday."

• • •

Elka makes spaghetti and meatballs and a big salad for dinner. You haven't had a frozen microwave meal in weeks.

"Have you seen your uncle today?" she asks.

Shake your head.

"It's strange, don't you think? For him to stay in his room all day. Not even to come out to eat."

Just then you hear the front door open and close, then footsteps on the gravel outside. A car door squeaks open, then slams shut. The car goes down the driveway. Weird. Uncle Lawrence has never left the house before without first saying good-bye.

He's not back by the time you go to bed. Lie awake in the dark, waiting, wondering. Sure enough, around three A.M. you hear the car. Peek through the blinds. Once again Uncle Lawrence, in his black jumpsuit, carries a heavy gym bag into the garage.

Minutes flit past. This time, when he comes out of the garage, he's dressed in regular clothes. He gets back into the car, then drives down the driveway. Heading back out at 3:12 A.M.

Out of Body

When you wake around noon the next day, the purple rental car is parked in the driveway. You wait until Uncle Lawrence gets up and leaves. Elka is out shopping. This is your chance. Stop at the front closet and pull on your winter parka. Outside, the air is dry and crisp. Your breath is a thick white vapor. In the garage, press the button to close the electric doors. Don't want anyone to see you.

Everything in the garage is in its place. Mountain bikes hang from hooks. Spades, trowels, rakes and shovels—all with matching yellow handles—hang from a sheet of brown Peg-Board. Green garden hoses are wrapped tightly around gray plastic storage spools. Work and gardening gloves lay neatly stacked on a shelf.

Search around and under your parents' cars. Check the shelves. Move the old golf bag out of the way. Those athletic bags have to be here somewhere. What about the large white buckets of pool chemicals? Uncle Lawrence mentioned that one of his jobs was pool maintenance. On the shelf is a pair of industrial-strength black rubber gloves. Press your nose close to them. A faint whiff of chlorine.

Pull the gloves on and start to work your fingers around the top of one of the pails, slowly prying off the lid. That's when the electric garage door opener starts to whir.

Quick. Duck behind the white plastic pails just as the Volvo pulls in. The concrete floor chills your legs and hands. The scents of pool chemicals and motor oil are in your nose.

The Volvo's engine stops. Hold your breath. The car's door creaks open, followed by the scratchy sound of feet and the crinkling of plastic grocery bags. Then footsteps cross the gravel driveway. In the distance the front door opens and closes.

Raise your head and look. Elka left the garage door open, but now you're partly hidden by the Volvo. Stay low. Pull the top off the white pail. Inside are bluish white crystals. The chemical stench stings your nose and burns your eyes. Dig a gloved hand down until the tips of your fingers hit something firm. Using both hands, paw the crystals aside. Under them is a clear plastic bag. Inside it is a black gym bag.

Scoop out handfuls of crystals. Pile them neatly into the top of the pail. Pull out the clear plastic bag.

With shaking fingers undo the wire twist, take out the gym bag and unzip it. Inside is a white letter-size envelope thick with fifty- and hundred-dollar bills. A plastic Ziploc bag filled with gold coins. Lying loose on the bottom are gold necklaces and bracelets studded with shimmering diamonds, pearls and green emeralds.

You have a strange, almost out-of-body experience. As if you're not really in your garage, at your house, in your world. You must be in a movie. This can't be real. Real life is boring and dull. Things like this don't happen in real life.

Pick up one of the gold bracelets. Tiny initials are carved on the inside: *SR.* Those initials are also inside a ring. Close the bag. Put everything back the way you found it. Now what?

Later. The house is dark. Elka's given you dinner and gone to her room to watch TV. Uncle Lawrence's car is still gone. Tiptoe down the stairs. Light each step with a small penlight. Your heart is beating hard and you're taking short, quick breaths. Poke the screwdriver through the hole in the doorknob, turn it slowly until you hear the click. Push the door open. The hinge squeaks. The room is dark. Following the small beam from the penlight, you discover a stack of newspapers piled neatly on the floor.

Search under the bed and in the closet. Then try the bureau.

Slide your hands under the clothes in each drawer and feel along the bottom. You're perfectly aware of how wrong this is, but you can't help yourself.

Bingo! In the back of the bottom drawer, you feel something. A small spiral notebook, not unlike the ones you use in school. Each page is dated, and the dates start almost exactly when Uncle Lawrence first moved in. The handwriting is crude, just like in the Christmas card.

CHANDLERS
WILLOW PATH

LE BICYCLETTE RESTAURANT. JASON WELLS, BARTENDER. SAYS THE CHANDLERS ARE FRIENDS OF THE OWNER. EAT THERE MOST SATURDAY NIGHTS.

ANTON CHANDLER, RETIRED BUILDING CONTRACTOR. GAMBLER. FREQUENT TRIPS TO VEGAS, A.C., CARIBBEAN. ALWAYS PAYS WITH CASH. DRIVES NEW JAGUAR. THOUGHT TO HAVE PAID CASH. WIFE JANICE HAS MAJOR JEWELS. BIG CASH TIPS TO HELP AT CHRISTMAS.

GATED DRIVEWAY. SECURITY CAMERAS. REMOTE ACCESS.

Flip ahead to another page.

MARCONI
RED STONE RD.

KEVIN PETERSEN GARDENER CONFIRMS HEAVY CASH FLOW. MARCONI DOESN'T REPORT IT ALL TO IRS.

MANUEL MARCONI OWNS MARCONI'S RESTAURANT. VERY POPULAR PLACE. EMPLOYEES PAID IN CASH. MANUEL RINGS OUT CASH REGISTER 11:30 P.M. EACH NIGHT (12:30 ON FRIDAYS/SATURDAYS). DRIVES STRAIGHT HOME. BANKS THURSDAY, MOSTLY DEPOSITS CHECKS. CASH APPEARS TO STAY SOMEWHERE IN HOUSE.

NO VISIBLE SIGN OF SECURITY SYSTEM. KEEPS TWO DOBERMANS.

Then another page:

REYNOLDS
7 OAK DRIVE

JACKIE ROWAN, COOKS FOR THE REYNOLDS ON OAK DRIVE. SAYS THEY GO SOUTH FOR THREE MONTHS AFTER CHRISTMAS.

JOSEPH AND SARAH REYNOLDS, ART AND ANTIQUITIES COLLECTORS. SOME PERSONAL JEWELRY. SUBSTANTIAL STOCK AND BOND PORTFOLIO.

WALL SAFE IN BEDROOM. ALSO LOCKED FILE CABINET IN DEN. POSSIBLE LOCK BOX IN BASEMENT.

CENTRAL STATION SECURITY SYSTEM. FIRST-FLOOR WINDOWS AND MOTION DETECTOR.

Wait a minute. Sarah Reynolds. *SR*. The initials in the jewelry you found. Oak Drive, Red Stone Road and Willow Path are all right here in Deep Meadow. On the next page is something different:

TOWN POLICE PATROL ON REVOLVING 8-DAY SCHEDULE ADVANCING HALF HOURS. SCHEDULE FOR CHRISTMAS– NEW YEAR'S

	OAK DRIVE	WILLOW PATH	RED STONE RD.
MONDAY	10:45	12 MIDNIGHT	1:25 A.M.
TUESDAY	11:15	12:30	1:55
WEDNESDAY	11:45	1 A.M.	2:25
THURSDAY	12:15	1:30	2:55
FRIDAY	12:45	2	3:25
SATURDAY	1:15	2:30	3:55
SUNDAY	1:45	3 A.M.	4:25

Put the notebook back in the drawer. Reach behind the window curtain. Find the voice-activated digital recorder. Now get out of there.

Detective Work

n your room, on the Internet, search the archives of newspapers from Tucson, Arizona, home to Arizona State University and former home to a phantom named Stuart Barnes. Use the following search terms: *thief* and *burglar.*

It's 3:17 A.M. You're feeling bleary. Eyelids want to come crashing down. About ready to give up the search. You've read through about a thousand burglary stories, but none makes you think Uncle Lawrence was involved. There's just one paper left, the *Sun Weekly.*

Its website is so slow, you almost fall asleep waiting for it to load. But the good thing about a weekly newspaper is that you only have to search through one-seventh as many stories as a daily. In no time you've worked your way back to September.

And there it is, in the September tenth issue:

THIEF SWEEPS THROUGH LA PALOMA ESTATES

Residents of this exclusive gated community had a nasty shock when they returned home last week after the long Labor Day holiday. Their expensive homes had been carefully burglarized by what local police call "one very smart thief."

"This was a well-planned, well-executed, professional job," said Detective Richard Skell of the Catalina police department. Four homes were burglarized. The thief managed to enter and leave without tripping alarm systems.

Detective Skell said the exact amount of goods stolen is still not known, but that the thief focused on cash and jewelry and other "small, easy to sell" items.

"The individual who perpetrated these break-ins obviously studied this area for quite a while," said Detective Skell. "He figured out how to get into a walled and gated community undetected. He knew who was going to be away for the weekend."

Detective Skell said the police were search-

> ing for leads, and asked that anyone with any information please call the Catalina PD.
>
> A source in the police department said that right now "the police have very little to go on. This individual was extremely good at covering his tracks. You naturally assume someone this good was using a fake ID. Even if we eventually figure out who this person was, you can bet he's long gone by now and operating under a whole new identity."

Hit print. Listen to the printer hum. Sit there until the screen saver comes on. It's one you loaded from a *Matrix* site—the black screen with the endlessly cascading green numbers. Only you don't see the numbers now. All you see is your reflection on the screen. Look at one of the few people on earth who knows the real name of that thief.

In bed you can't sleep. Heart thumping; stomach queasy. You wanted proof? You got it. Uncle Lawrence is a professional thief and he's been stealing from homes right here in Deep Meadow. It doesn't take a genius to figure out why he has a stack of newspapers in his room. He wants to know if any of his burglaries have been reported yet.

Lie in the dark. Wonder what to do next. Remember the voice-activated recorder. Flick on the light and sit up with your back against the headboard. The recorder in your trembling fingers. Press play.

Learn the following information about Uncle Lawrence: He snores. Also yawns, grunts and sometimes groans.

Did you really expect him to suddenly announce to no one in particular: "I'm a crook! I rob houses! In Lake Tahoe they called me the Dinnertime Thief!"

Dumb, Martin. Truly feeble.

But then, on the recorder, a whisper: *"Hi. . . . Nice to hear your voice, too. . . . We're still on for tomorrow night, right? . . . What? Why not? . . . Come on, Idahlia, Martin's a good kid. Even if he knew, I don't think he'd say anything."*

What is this?

"You know how I feel about you. . . . I know, I know. . . . No, I do understand. But I also understand that this is something special. . . . Yes, I know you feel that, too."

You can't help smiling to yourself.

"Idahlia, can I be honest with you? It's been a long time since I felt this way about anyone. A really long time. I don't know what it means, but I just can't take no for an answer. Of course I know you're a professional. I wouldn't—" Rap! Rap!

Sounds like knocking on a door. Uncle Lawrence's voice drops: *"Hold on."* Then louder: *"Just a minute."*

Sounds like the other day when you knocked on his door to remind him that he was taking you to Dr. Rodriguez's. On the recorder, your uncle's voice is barely a whisper: *"Oh, come on, sure you can. . . . Who's going to know? . . . There's no law against it. . . . What? Maybe you'll see me sooner than you think."*

Click. The recording ends.

So, his honey's name is Idahlia. You stiffen. In a flash you're out of bed. Cross the upstairs hall to Mom's study. On her desk is a Rolodex. The kind with the slits in the pages for business cards. Quickly flip through the R's to:

By Appointment
833-0676

Idahlia Rodriguez, Ph.D.
LICENSED PSYCHOLOGIST

Suite 312
2065 Grand Ave.

Leaving

O pen your eyes and squint. Your bedroom is filled with sunlight. Not that low, slanting morning light either. This is bright middle-of-the-day glare.

Uncle Lawrence . . . Just the thought of him instantly makes your heart race and fills you with anxious, twisted sensations. He's broken into homes right here in your neighborhood. *What should you do?* Call the police? Or your parents? Turn him in?

You've missed breakfast. Maybe lunch, too. Couldn't eat right now anyway. Your stomach has posted a no-trespassing sign. What to do? You know what you're *supposed* to do. Or, at least, *you think* you know. You're supposed to tell. He's breaking the law. This isn't a video game.

But it isn't a school shooting either.

Uncle Lawrence is your friend. Your father's brother. Yes, he's breaking the law. But it's not like he's really hurting anyone, is he? Will you keep his secret? Pretend you don't know?

No! You *do* know. The jewelry and cash. The notes about security systems and local police patrol schedules. The fake IDs and night-vision scope. It all makes sense now. Going out at night to study their houses and police patrol schedules. Don't deny it, Martin. You *know.*

And what about Dr. Rodriguez?

Spend most of the day in your room. Elka comes by and you tell her you're just being lazy. The hours pass. The light outside slowly backs away and evaporates into gray. Night arrives. All you see in the window are reflections against a black background.

What should you do?

Does Dr. Rodriguez know what Uncle Lawrence is?

Nearly midnight and difficult to stay awake. Play computer games. Blink a lot. Try to stay focused. Double gravity kicks in. Your arms feel heavy and it's an effort to keep your head up.

Open your eyes. You've been sleeping at your desk with your head on your arms. Your face only inches from the computer, bathed in the green glow of the *Matrix* screen saver. Thin streams of symbols fall in an endless numerical waterfall. Your eye goes to the clock: 3:32 A.M. From the dark outside comes the sound of footsteps. Part the blinds. No moonlight glow tonight, just the lights from the house creeping across the driveway to silhouette the rental car. Uncle Lawrence carries two heavy athletic bags, one in each hand, from the garage to the car. He's wearing his long leather coat.

Groggy and half asleep, your brain is slow to fire up. *That's why he came with so little . . . because he planned to leave with so much . . .*

Push your chair back and stagger to your feet. Downstairs, open the closet and pull out a parka. Outside it's like stepping into a freezer; the crisp, frigid air jolts your lungs. The driveway pebbles are hard and icy underfoot. You remembered the parka, but forgot the shoes.

Uncle Lawrence looks up quickly. His face shadowy. Lips pressed together in a hard, thin line.

"Go back inside." Almost a growl, shrouded in a gray cloud of vapor. A tone of voice you've never heard from him before. Icy. Threatening.

"No." Heart racing at a sickening, fearful pace. You could throw up. Only it's not food you're holding down. "I know what you are! I figured it out."

Uncle Lawrence doesn't move, but his eyes go about as large and round as you've ever seen them.

"I'm sorry. I mean, I wish I didn't know. Really. I'd do *anything* not to know."

Still as a statue, Uncle Lawrence watches you uncertainly. Like you're a stranger. Or worse, the enemy. Deadly serious. "What are you going to do, Martin?"

"I don't know. Just don't go."

He looks past you at the house. You turn to see, but no one's there. Just the dark outline of the walls and roof.

"I have to go," he says.

"No!"

Uncle Lawrence winces. "Keep it *down*."

Lower your voice. "You *can* stay."

Your uncle's sigh is a cloud of white. "They're looking for me."

"The police? They know it's you?"

"Not yet. But they will if I stick around."

"Why can't you stay and just give everything back?"

He smiles in the dark. The smile says, *You don't know what you're talking about. You're just a kid.*

"So you're just going to go? I mean, forever?"

"It's that or the big house."

"Big house?"

"Prison."

Feel the tears welling up in your eyes. "No. You can't go."

He gazes at you long and hard in the dark. As if he's actually thinking about it. Then he closes his eyes, shakes his head one last time, turns and gets into the car.

No Tricks

The rental car's engine starts. Uncle Lawrence twists around in the driver's seat to look out the rear window. The car backs down the driveway.

He's going.

He's a thief. He got you to like him and now he's taking that away.

Leaving you with nothing.

Grab the door handle. Still looking out the rear window, your uncle doesn't know you're there. The car keeps backing up. Hold on and jog alongside. Your bare feet cry in pain as they land on the cold, odd-shaped pebbles.

Uncle Lawrence swivels around and sees you. Hits the brakes. The car stops. He rolls down the window. "Let go!" Sharp. Angry.

"No."

Clenched teeth. "What do you want?"

"To go with you."

"Are you—?" Catches himself. "You're just a kid, Doc."

"So?"

"You can't come."

"Why not?"

"I told you to let go."

"Not till you tell me why I can't come."

Uncle Lawrence grits his teeth. You expect him to yell. Instead he looks away.

"My parents left you in charge of me. You can't be in charge of me if you go. So either you stay or I go with you."

"Shut. Up." Uncle Lawrence growls. He's grimly angry. You're scared. Reminds you of your father. You do as you're told, but your hand stays tight around the door handle.

You expect the car to start backing away again, but it doesn't. Seconds pass. Uncle Lawrence sits there, hands on the steering wheel, staring straight ahead. Somewhere in the dark, the early bird chirps. It must be 3:45 A.M. That's the *way* early bird.

Your uncle looks up. "Okay, get in."

Don't let go of the door handle. "No tricks?"

He rolls his eyes. "No tricks, Doc."

Walk around *behind* the car just to make sure he doesn't try a fast getaway. Pull open the passenger door. Slide into the seat. Grin at your uncle.

He shakes his head wearily. Starts to back down the driveway again.

Big Feet

D rive down vast stretches of dark highway. Not another car in sight. Just broken white lines, and now and then a thin curtain of mist. Green exit signs grow larger, brighter, then vanish. Gray concrete overpasses appear and disappear. Your body is stretchy tired, but your mind is clear. Must be the adrenaline. You're not sure why, but you're happy.

"Where are we going?" you ask.

"Does it matter?" Your uncle, on the other hand, is clearly *not* happy.

In the distance across the misty highway median, the headlights of a truck approach, the top of the cab and the trailer outlined with small amber lights.

"Know what the amber ones are called?" you ask.

"No, but I bet you do."

"Clearance lights."

Uncle Lawrence shifts his position in the driver's seat.

"Think it's dumb, right?" you ask.

"No, I don't think it's dumb. I'm thinking about what to do with you."

"Take me with you. We'll be a team."

"Don't be stupid!" he snaps angrily.

Ow! That stung. You slouch down in the seat. Now he *really* sounds like your father. Except he takes a deep breath and lets it go slowly. "Sorry, Doc. You're not stupid. You're interesting. An interesting kid."

Your father would never apologize. The sting ebbs more quickly than you expect. You sense Uncle Lawrence didn't really mean it. He's just nervous, worried, maybe even scared. Deep down he likes you. Your eyelids feel heavy. Keep talking. Try to stay awake.

"You're not *really* mad, are you?"

"Not really. Stuff happens. You live with it."

"Can I ask you a question?"

Uncle Lawrence shoots you a glance. Like he needs a moment to prepare himself because he knows it's going to be a zinger. "Oh, okay."

"Why do you have to steal?"

A tiny yellow spot appears far off to your right. It slowly grows larger and more distinct and becomes the golden arches of a McDonald's near an exit. You're well past it before Uncle Lawrence answers.

"It's what I'm good at, Doc."

"Be serious."

"I *am* serious. You know your dad. He had to be the best. Had to beat me at everything. Sports, school, socially, girls, you name it. I was the why-can't-you-be-more-like-your-brother kid. The only thing I did better than him was steal."

"Did someone teach you?"

Uncle Lawrence chuckles and shakes his head like he can't believe how dumb your question is.

"What's so funny?" you ask.

"You just learn. I had a talent for it, I guess. Even used to practice. Your father would shoot basketballs. I'd see how much I could take without getting caught."

"But it's wrong."

"Everything I did was wrong."

"That doesn't make it right."

"Hey, I know that, okay? I . . . I don't know. If I could do it over again, I'm pretty sure I'd do it differently."

You yawn. "It's not too late." Suddenly you feel very tired.

Open your eyes and squint into daylight. Neck stiff from sleeping in the car. A roaring sound comes from somewhere close. Tart traces of burnt jet fuel in your nose. Uncle Lawrence drives slowly past a long row of similar-looking red and green cars. Their windows and bodies covered with a dull gauze of early morning dew.

Yawn and stretch. "Where are we?"

"Airport."

"We going somewhere?"

"No."

Disappointment crashes down. You're ready to go. Doesn't matter where. Who'd really miss you?

Park in front of a yellow-and-black Hertz office. Inside an agent sits at the empty counter, drinking coffee from a paper cup.

"Let's go." Uncle Lawrence gets out. You push open the door. The concrete sidewalk feels cold and rough under your bare feet. Stretch your legs for the first time in hours. Still bleary from lack of sleep. Your uncle goes around to the trunk. Takes out the black athletic bags, the carry-on, milk crates, telescope, and finally the silver case, which he lowers to the sidewalk with a thud.

"You can wait—" he begins, then goes quiet. Stares at your feet.

You shrug. "Forgot my shoes."

He squats down and unzips the carry-on. Pulls out a pair of tennis shoes. "Try these."

Even without socks they're tight. Your toes jam up against the fronts.

Uncle Lawrence makes a face. "I thought you said those basketball shoes I gave you fit."

"They were a little small," you admit.

He rubs his chin. "Not that I'm an expert or anything, but based on those feet, I'd bet you're going to be a lot taller than your father. Now, wait here."

"And don't let anyone near this stuff?"

"You got it, Doc."

Mr. Heartbreaker

He gets into the car and drives away. You wait on the sidewalk with the bags. The orange sun is rising, its rays feel warm. The fuzzy patches of dew on the parked cars begin to shrink. Small islands of shiny red or green appear on the hoods and gradually grow.

A lot taller than your father? Hard to believe. Sure hope it's truc.

A little while later Uncle Lawrence drives up in a white car, gets out, begins to load in the athletic bags. You reach for the carry-on to help, but Uncle Lawrence picks it up first.

"That's okay, Doc. Just get in."

It smells new and has the bare look of a rental. Uncle Lawrence gets in and starts to drive.

"How come you switched cars?"

"Didn't like the color." He follows the blue-and-red signs back toward the highway.

"Where are we going?" you ask.

"Home."

"I don't want to go home. I want to go with you."

"Sorry, kid." Uncle Lawrence talks funny, out of the side of his mouth. "Where I'm going, you can't follow. What I've got to do, you can't be any part of."

"What's that from?"

"A movie. *Casablanca.*"

"Was that guy a thief, too?"

"Uh, no."

"Why can't you do something else?"

"Like what? Drive a cab? Be a bartender? I don't want to do that kind of stuff. I *can't* do that kind of stuff."

"Because of my dad?"

"I guess. I know it's a weird, twisted way to find self-respect, but it's true."

"It's wrong."

Uncle Lawrence gives you that look.

"Right." You remember. "Everything you did was wrong."

"I made some mistakes when I was younger. Got into trouble. If you don't finish high school, *and* you make a few mistakes, it kind of limits your options."

"As far as getting a job?"

Your uncle nods.

"There is something else you could do."

"What's that?" he asks.

"Be someone's dad."

Uncle Lawrence's mouth twists in a funny way. Like he doesn't know whether you're kidding him or not.

"I'm serious. You're about a hundred times more patient and fun and understanding than my father."

"That's not all there is to it," Uncle Lawrence says. "You have to know how to raise a kid. How to teach them right from wrong and make sure they understand the value of hard work."

"There you go. You just told me all the things you need to do."

He shakes his head. "You can't be a thief and have a family. You can't move a kid every couple of months."

"Who said you'd have to move?"

"It's that or the big house."

"There's another way."

"What's that?"

"Stop stealing."

"Right." Uncle Lawrence chuckles bitterly. "I'm going to stop stealing, get married, settle down and raise a family."

"Why not?"

"You're a smart kid, Doc. Smart enough that sometimes I forget that you're only thirteen."

"That hurts."

"I'm just trying to explain. There's a lot you don't know."

"I'm still waiting for one good reason why you couldn't do it."

"What would I do for money?" Uncle Lawrence asks. "I mean, if anything I'd have to steal twice as much because I'd have a wife and a kid."

"Maybe your wife would work. You could take care of the kid."

"And just where am I going to find this amazing woman?"

"Dr. Rodriguez."

The car actually swerves. Tires hum harshly on the rough asphalt at the edge of the highway.

"Hey, watch it!" you yelp.

Your uncle steers back into the lane, clears his throat. "You continue to surprise me."

"You're just going to go away forever and not tell her?"

"Careful, Doc," he cautions.

"Don't you think this is going to hurt her, too?"

"It won't be the first time."

"Oh, Mr. Heartbreaker over here."

Uncle Lawrence smirks. "You crack me up."

"Only I'm serious. She really likes you."

"I won't ask how you know that."

"But it's true, right?"

He takes a deep breath and lets it out slowly. "Yes, I believe it is."

"Don't you like her?"

"Yes, Doc, I do."

. . .

Somewhere near Deep Meadow, Uncle Lawrence pulls into the parking lot of a diner with mirrored windows and red and gold Merry Christmas letters on the door.

"Hungry?" he asks.

"Always."

"Let's get you something to eat." He starts to open his door.

"Wait."

He gives you a curious look. "What?"

"You don't ever hurt people, do you?"

Your uncle kind of snorts and shakes his head. "No. That's all TV stuff. If you're smart and disciplined, you don't have to hurt anyone."

"And besides, you don't have a gun."

"How . . . ?" Then he grins. "Oh, right, because I was so bad at Double Tap?"

"The worst."

"Don't rub it in, okay?"

"The antigun burglar. That's a first."

"Look, you want to make fun of me or eat?"

"Can't I do both?"

The two of you laugh. You really like Uncle Lawrence. You really, really do.

The sun is higher, but the early morning air still carries a chill. Inside the diner, men wearing down vests and women in polar fleeces sit in booths, eating breakfast. Some read newspapers. Some smoke and talk.

Uncle Lawrence leads you to the counter. "Have a seat, order whatever you want. I'll be right back."

A waitress hands you a menu. Out in the vestibule, your uncle makes a call from the pay phone. You realize he doesn't have a cell phone. Then again, cell phone calls can be traced.

You order pancakes, orange juice and hot chocolate. Uncle Lawrence comes back, but doesn't sit down.

"Want a menu?" the waitress asks him.

"No, thanks."

You turn to him. "Not eating?"

"Gotta go, Doc." He places a twenty-dollar bill on the counter, then pats your shoulder. "This'll cover breakfast and the cab home. He'll be here in about twenty minutes, okay?"

Shake your head. "No, not okay."

Uncle Lawrence's shoulders sag. "Look, Doc, try to understand."

"No." In about a nanosecond you go from feeling good to feeling bad. So bad, you feel tears well up in your eyes.

He puts a hand on your shoulder. "I promise I'll be in touch one day. Your dad and I manage to see each other every couple of years, right?"

Nod, even though you don't want to wait a couple of years. Uncle Lawrence makes a fist and holds it out. You tap his knuckles with yours.

"You're a great kid, Doc." He turns toward the door.

Nothing you can do will prevent him from going. But there is something you want to say.

"My father's wrong."

Uncle Lawrence stops and looks back at you.

"You don't have to be the best," you tell him. "Just because my father makes you *feel* that way. It's not your problem. It's his. There's a difference between *doing* the best *you* can, and *being* better than everyone else."

Your uncle just gazes at you. "Thanks, Doc." Once again, he turns to go. Once again he stops. "If anyone asks, what color car was I driving?"

Look out at the white rental car in the parking lot. "A dark red convertible with a black top."

He winks. "You're a good kid."

"So I've been told."

He holds out his fist and you tap knuckles again. "I'm going to miss you, Doc. And I would have beaten you in Double Tap."

"Not a chance."

"Hey, you're the one who said if you keep trying, you can do anything, right?"

"Almost."

He forces a small sad smile. Knows in a second he's going to walk out of that door and you may never see him again. Knows he'll miss you just like you'll miss him. Jam your hands into the pockets of your parka. Feel the Swiss Army knife.

"Here." Hold it out toward him.

"Why?" he asks.

"It'll make your job easier."

He takes the knife and weighs it in his hand. Raising and lowering his palm as if judging its value. "Thanks, Doc."

He turns and walks out of the diner, across the parking lot to the car. Before he gets in, he waves. You wave back, but doubt he can see you through the mirrored windows.

The cab drops you at home just before 8:00 A.M. Tiptoe inside. Elka isn't in the kitchen yet. Go to your room, get into bed and quickly fall asleep.

Later you wake to the sound of voices. Stumble down the stairs in a T-shirt and pajama bottoms. Your parents are there—in their coats, amid their brown briefcases and black luggage. Mom spreads her arms and pulls you into a hug. The scent of stale perfume and jet planes fills your nose. Your father rubs your head. He's smiling and seems genuinely happy to see you.

"I missed you too much," Mom blurts as she smothers you in her arms. "I'm never going away for that long again."

"I think you've gotten taller," adds your father.

Without letting go, Mom pulls back to look at you. "And what's this?" She touches your upper lip. "You're starting to get a moustache." She turns to your father. "I think it's time you showed him how to shave."

Shave? The word is a slam dunk to your ears. You the man! Stand tall. Feels like you beat Double Tap on one token. Like you just killed a tree ten times the size of the one in your living room. The Paul Bunyan of Deep Meadow!

Your father steps closer and squints at your face. "You can barely see it."

On the other hand, you couldn't cut a toothpick with a power saw, you hairless wimp.

"Well, it wouldn't hurt to show him how anyway," goes Mom. She glances around. "How is Elka?"

"She's been great. She must be out shopping."

"And my brother?" asks your father.

"He left."

They both scowl at you.

"When?" asks Mom.

"Uh, this morning."

Mom turns to your father. "Why would he leave without saying good-bye?"

Your father lets his hands flop against his sides. "Who knows? And anyway, we're back. So what does it matter?"

Thanks Anyway

On the floor outside Dr. Rodriguez's door the sound machine whirs. Thumb through a *Time* magazine from a month ago. The door opens and the world's most beautiful babe psychologist scans the waiting room.

"He's gone," you tell her.

Her face goes blank. "Please come in."

Dr. Rodriguez takes her regular seat and pulls the hem of her skirt down over her knees. You pick up the yellow Nerf ball and try to squeeze it down to almost nothing in your fist.

"How are you?" she asks.

"He's not coming back."

"How does that make you feel?"

"How does it make *you* feel?" you shoot back.

"You're angry."

"No duh."

"You liked him and now you feel betrayed."

"Don't you?"

Dr. Rodriguez goes quiet.

More gently, you add, "You liked him, too. Don't deny it."

"Did he say where he was going?"

"No."

"Why?"

Hand her a folded-up article from the newspaper about the burglaries in Deep Meadow over Christmas vacation. Police are quoted about how "professional" the thief was. Dr. Rodriguez unfolds and scans it. Looks up at you. "I don't understand."

"It's him."

She looks down, takes longer to read it this time. "What makes you think so?"

Hand her the story you printed from the Tucson *Sun Weekly*. Wait for her to read it. Then hand her one more sheet of paper. A photocopy of Uncle Lawrence's fake IDs.

Dr. Rodriguez goes pale. Slowly refolds the papers you've given her. "You're sure?"

"I'm Mr. Observant, remember?"

She doesn't smile. Only gazes at some spot on the ceiling. Touches the place on her finger where there's only a ghost of a ring now. Her eyes begin to glisten. Looks away and blinks a couple of times.

"You okay?" you ask.

She gives you a crooked smile. "Yes, Martin. Thank

you for asking." But the words are hardly through her lips when the smile crumbles and the tears spill out of her eyes. She quickly reaches for a tissue and dabs them. Blows her nose and does a fast mop-up job. She tries to establish eye contact with you again, but she can't do it. Her eyes once again fill with tears and she reaches for another tissue.

Normally a patient in a psychologist's office might find this display of emotion shocking. But you understand completely. "Maybe I should go wait outside, huh?"

Dr. Rodriguez blows her nose and nods. "If . . . you wouldn't mind. Thank you, Martin."

Blue and red lights flash through the trees in the darkness. Elka parks on the side of the road because a police car is blocking the entrance to your driveway. You've just gotten out of your car when two sedans come down from your house. The first has a flashing red light on the dashboard. Two men sit in the front and one in the back. Their faces briefly bathed in red each time the dashboard beam revolves. Just enough light for you to see that Uncle Lawrence is in the backseat. You feel a dizzy, sickening jolt. From the way his arms are pulled behind him, you know he's handcuffed.

The first sedan squeezes past the patrol car blocking the entrance. Uncle Lawrence stares straight ahead, but as the car passes, he becomes aware of you. Silently you greet each other through the side window. The skin around your uncle's eyes wrinkles with shame and defeat.

The dark sedan turns out of the driveway, followed by the white rental car Uncle Lawrence was driving when he left you at the diner. A police officer is behind the wheel now. The two cars head away and disappear around a tree-lined curve.

Stand in the damp, cold dark, shivering. *Why did you come back, Uncle Lawrence?*

Feel a hand on your shoulder. It's Elka. "Come, Martin, they say we can go in."

Ride in silence up the driveway. Strange that Elka doesn't ask what you think has happened. Maybe she just assumes you wouldn't know.

Yet another sedan is parked in front of your house. The two men inside appear to be writing in notebooks. One looks up briefly, nods at you, then goes back to writing. You and Elka go into the house and you go into your room. The Swiss Army knife is lying on your computer keyboard. What's it doing here? A small note, carefully folded, sticks out of the space between the pliers and the scissors. It's in that same terrible handwriting.

> DOC,
>   GUESS I WON'T BE NEEDING THIS AFTER ALL.
> THANKS ANYWAY.
>
>   —LAWRENCE

You hear a car coming up the driveway too fast. It's Mom. The station wagon skids to a stop, noisily spraying gravel. She jumps out and hurries toward the house. Front door opens and slams. Footsteps up the stairs. Your bedroom door opens and she comes in. Eyes red-rimmed from crying. Takes two quick steps, then slows herself down, stops and places her hands on your shoulders.

"It's okay, Mom."

"No, Martin. It's not okay." She squeezes your shoulders. "Your father and I did something terrible. We left you home with . . . well, for lack of a better word . . . a criminal. Because we thought our work was more important."

"You didn't know."

"A parent should have," she insists. "A parent shouldn't leave a child with *anyone* unless they're sure . . . positive beyond a shadow of a doubt. We didn't do that. We grabbed the first person we could find and dashed out the door."

"But it worked out okay."

"What if you'd been home when the police arrived? He might have taken you hostage."

"No way. He'd never do that. And anyway, he couldn't take me hostage. He doesn't even have a gun."

Mom starts to say something, then stops as if she's just been struck. She leans forward. "How do you know that?"

"He told me."

"He *told* you he didn't have a gun."

Uh-oh. You see where she's going with this. But it's too late. You've just admitted that you knew Uncle Lawrence was a thief *before* he was caught.

From outside comes the sound of tires again. It's Dad's Mercedes. Mom sets her jaw. "Excuse me." She leaves your room.

Over the intercom, listen to the worst fight your parents have ever had. In the end, life has changed. From now on, Mom is working from home.

Dog-Breath Torture

D ude, you're famous!" It's lunchtime in Cyberia and Wendell has the local newspaper. Sits down in your igloo and points at the front-page headline:

THIEF CAUGHT!

Below it, a color photo of Uncle Lawrence, his head bowed to avoid the camera and his hands cuffed behind him. Escorted by two men in dark suits. The caption says they're leading him into jail.

Experience dog-breath torture. Luckily you've come prepared. Take out a brand-new tin of Altoids and offer Wendell as many as he wants. He pops two into his mouth. *Relief!* You can actually listen without covering your nose when he starts to read: "A call from a security alarm company on Tuesday led to the arrest of a thief blamed for a number of local burglaries in the exclusive

Deep Meadow Estates area. Police said the thief, whose identity is still not known, was arrested in the home of Evan and Rebecca Hunter—"

He looks up from the newspaper. "Your parents, right?"

"Never heard of them."

Wendell gives you a goofy grin, then starts reading again: "—home of Evan and Rebecca Hunter after tripping a silent alarm. The Hunters were not at home at the time. Police said evidence found at the scene linked the thief to at least three other recent burglaries during the Christmas holidays.

" 'This guy is a real pro,' reported Detective Andrew Dobronyi. 'He got past the security systems in the first three houses he hit, and didn't leave a clue. We just got lucky.' "

Wendell keeps reading, but you don't really hear any more. *"Lucky"?* you're thinking. *If only they really knew . . .*

Dr. Rodriguez's eyes are darkly ringed and have a hollow, sunken look. You and she sit for a long time without talking. What's weird is you're certain that you are both thinking about the same thing.

"He changed his mind," you finally say. "He came back and tripped the alarm on purpose."

The faint lines in Dr. Rodriguez's forehead deepen. "Why?"

"He didn't want to be a thief anymore. He isn't a bad person. He knew what he did was wrong. He stole because it was the only thing he did well."

More silence creeps into the office. It's how people react when they don't believe you. If they think you're lying on purpose, they get mad. If they think you're totally wrong but you really believe what you're saying, they just look sad. Dr. Rodriguez presses her lips into a crooked line that dips down in both corners. Her eyes go soft, almost pitying you.

"I'm serious," you insist.

"I know."

"Then why don't you believe me?"

"If he changed his mind, why didn't he go to the police and turn himself in?"

"I think he planned to. That's why he had all the stuff he took in his car. I think he was going to do it, but first he had to give me something."

She cocks her head in a questioning look.

"A Swiss Army knife. It's a long story."

Dr. Rodriguez thinks for a moment, then crosses her arms as if she's made a decision. "He's a criminal, Martin." Her voice is cold and firm.

"No, not *really*. I mean, I know what he did was wrong, but he didn't think he had a choice."

"Everyone has a choice. I'm sorry, Martin, but there is no excuse for breaking the law."

Famous

Instead of school the next morning, you are at the Deep Meadow police station with your father and a lawyer named Mr. Shrag. Shrag has a square face, small blue eyes and short reddish hair. Wears a dark gray suit, a pressed blue shirt with a white collar and a yellow tie. He is built like one of those big boxes TVs come in. For some strange reason he reminds you of a bulldozer.

You and Shragdozer sit in a small room with grimy yellow walls and the permanent odor of cigarettes. Detective Clark, a thin bald man in a rumpled brown suit, asks you questions about Uncle Lawrence, but Shragdozer gives all the answers. After twenty minutes Detective Clark says you both can leave. Outside the room, your father is waiting on a wooden bench.

"How did it go?" he asks anxiously.

Shragdozer puts his meaty hand on your shoulder. "He did great."

"I didn't do anything." You shrug his hand off.

Shragdozer turns to your father. "Ready?"

"Ready."

They go back into the room, leaving you in the hall on the wooden bench.

Clank! From the other end of the hallway comes the dull bang of metal meeting metal. *A cell door closing?* Lean forward and crane your neck to see if it's Uncle Lawrence.

"He ain't here."

Swivel around. A tall police officer with a blond moustache is standing in the doorway. *How could he know?* Realize the obvious. Everyone knows. Who else would you be looking for?

"He's been moved to the county lockup," the officer says.

Give him a puzzled look. He explains: "That's the jail. The county jail."

Mental note: Find out where the county jail is.

Get to school late. The halls are empty. Everyone's in class. You probably should have brought a note:

To whom it may concern:
Martin was late this morning because he had to
be questioned by the police.

Go to the attendance office and wait at the counter. A grandmother-type secretary with stiff blond hair looks up from her desk. "What can I do for you, young man?"

"Can I get a late pass?"

She reaches for the pad of blank late passes. "Name?"

"Martin Hunter."

She raises her head and squints at you. She knows.

Go to English. The door is closed, but through the window you see them and they see you. Mr. Hatch, your English teacher, instantly senses that no one's paying attention. He comes to the door and opens it. Hand him the late pass. He doesn't bother to read it. Head for your desk.

Everyone stares. Everyone knows. Wendell was right—you're famous.

At lunch you're still in Cyberia. Not because you have no place else to go, but because it's the only place where they don't gawk. Wendell waits at your igloo with the latest edition of the local paper, the one with the story revealing to the public for the first time that Lawrence is your father's brother. "That guy was your uncle?" Offer him two Altoids. Wendell takes them. "He lived with you for a month?"

Nod. Bite into the first school lunch your mother has ever prepared. Tuna with mayo and celery. Not quite enough mayo and the celery chunks are too big, but you believe you can work with her on this.

"Did you have any idea?" Wendell asks.

Shake your head even though it's not true. Shragdozer's orders. You cannot go around telling the world you knew your uncle was a thief.

The house smells like cinnamon. In the kitchen, Mom is wearing jeans, a blue shirt and red baking mitts that look like lobster claws. Like that lady on TV. "Hi, hon, milk and cookies?"

This is too weird for words. But, as usual, you're hungry. "Sure."

She pulls off the mitts, gets out the milk and Oreos. You're glad the cookies aren't homemade. It's strange enough that she's home at 3:30 in the afternoon, giving you a snack.

"How did you like your lunch?" she asks as she places a glass of milk and a plate of cookies on the table.

"Overall I gave it high marks. The bag of chips was a nice touch. Where's Elka?"

Mom goes back to the oven. "I gave her the day off."

"Heard anything about Uncle Lawrence?"

She gazes out the window.

"Mom? You know where the county jail is?"

She looks at you, her face creased with concern and worry. "Why do you want to know?"

"I thought maybe we should go see him."

"Your father and I will be seeing him. He'll have a very good lawyer. He's family and we'll do everything we can for him."

"What about me seeing him?"

She doesn't answer.

"You think he's a bad influence, right?"

She gives you a strange look. Mouth twisted half in a smile, half in a frown. Like she thinks your question is funny and sad at the same time. "He's a criminal, Martin. Yes, I'd say that makes him a bad influence."

Fight the temptation to argue. Eat a cookie instead. *Bing!* rings the white timer on the kitchen counter. Mom pulls a freshly baked loaf of cinnamon bread from the oven. Her cheeks are red and she's beaming. The kitchen fills with a warm doughy scent as she places the pan on the counter. "*Voilà!* Businesswoman bakes bread!" She picks up a knife. "Try a piece?"

"I think you're supposed to let it cool down first." You recall this detail from the time your kindergarten class baked rolls.

"Oh, okay." She puts down the knife.

"Mom, is this whole stay-at-home-and-bake-bread thing for real? I mean, you're not gonna do this for a week and then get bored and go back to work, are you?"

She slides off the baking mitts. "It's for real, Martin."

"I hope it's not totally because of me," you tell her. "Because I'm too old to have a mom at home."

"I understand," Mom agrees. "I'll just be here if you need me."

"For what?" you ask.

"Milk and cookies."

Ain't No Way

The arrest of your uncle is the biggest news to hit Deep Meadow since a couple of guys from the Public Works Department were caught stealing quarters from parking meters. Given how rare it is for anything exciting to happen here, the local newspaper tries to run a different story about Uncle Lawrence every day.

One story is about some other robberies that happened a few years ago and whether Uncle Lawrence could have been involved with those as well. Another story concerns the money and jewelry the police found in the trunk of Uncle Lawrence's car. The people whose houses were robbed are fighting over whom the loot really belongs to. They all claim most of it is theirs.

After a couple of weeks the flood of stories slows to a drip. Days pass with no mention of your uncle. All you know now is that he is in the county jail, awaiting trial.

"He's in good spirits," your mother reports after she and your father return from a visit.

"Since it's a first offense, Shrag is hoping Lawrence will get a light sentence," adds your father.

"Can't I come next time?" you ask. "I *know* he wants to see me, too."

Your parents exchange the old you-tell-him-no look. Forget it, kid. Ain't no way.

"You feel hurt and disappointed," Dr. Rodriguez observes when you bring this up in her office.

"How do you think *he* feels?" you shoot back. "Alone in jail with almost no one to talk to."

"Your parents see him."

"Yeah, right. Once every other week. And you know my father's the last person in the world he wants to see. Know who he wants to see? You, and me."

"How do you know?" she asks.

You're in no mood for niceties today. "You know it and I know it. He liked us. He wanted to do stuff with me even when he didn't have to."

"You've said that he was used to moving from place to place and leaving people behind," Dr. Rodriguez points out.

"He *was* used to it, but that doesn't mean he *liked* it. That's why he came back. He wanted to stop that old life."

"How can you be so sure?" she asks.

"Because he'd already gotten away. He had no reason to come back. Except for us. Only now he's been sitting in jail for nearly a month and he hasn't seen either of us. I bet he really regrets coming back now. I bet if he'd known it was going to be like this, he would have just kept going and *never* come back."

Copping a Plea

Another lunch in Cyberia. Wendell comes in. "Big day today, huh?"

"For what?"

He gives you a suspicious look—as if you're joking. "Didn't you see the paper?"

Shake your head. It's been a while since you checked the local paper. And it's not like your parents feel the need to fill you in on every little detail concerning Uncle Lawrence.

"He's gonna cop a plea."

"What's that?" Offer Wendell two Altoids. Does this guy *ever* brush his teeth?

Wendell pops them into his mouth. "Don't you watch TV? When you cop a plea, you plead guilty to a lesser crime. He and his lawyer are hoping the court will go easy on him but the good citizens of Deep Meadow are demanding he do hard time in state prison."

"When's it going to be decided?" you ask.

"Soon as he's sentenced. Today, I guess."

If he goes to state prison, you'll never see him again.

By now you've learned that the county court is in Newton, about twenty miles from Deep Meadow. Only, by the time school's over, it'll be too late.

Reach for your backpack. "I'm going."

"Uh, we're in school, remember?" Wendell reminds you.

Give him a look that cuts through the you-know-what.

"You serious?" he whispers. "Just gonna walk out the front door? Where all the office windows are? You'll be nailed instantly."

"I don't care."

"Listen, genius, what do we have next period?"

"Math . . ." You realize what he's getting at. The march of the brainiac Sherpas. The perfect excuse to leave school without getting in trouble.

Rain starts to fall from the gray clouds just as you and Wendell step outside. Drops of water spot your glasses.

"The bus stop's two blocks over on Palmer," Wendell says.

You take out your wallet. Inside are two one-dollar bills. Now that Mom makes your lunch every day, you're not in the habit of carrying more than a few dollars to school. Wendell sees this. Reaches into his pocket, pulls out a crumpled ten, hands it to you.

"That much?"

"Plan on coming back, don't you?"

The raindrops multiply and come down harder, pelting your shoulders and exploding at your feet. Cold ticklish rainwater runs out of your hair and down the sides of your neck. "Thanks. I owe you."

"Darn right." He holds out his fist and you tap knuckles. "Good luck."

Head off toward the bus stop while Wendell continues toward the high school. He's a good guy. Maybe he could even be a friend. As long as you keep him supplied with Altoids.

Surprise

The county courthouse is a marble fortress with tall white columns in front. The wide marble steps are glossy-slick with rainwater. Your wet hair is plastered down on your head and your scalp is chilled. Icy drops creep under your shirt collar and down the middle of your back. They tickle and make you shiver.

Walk between the columns and push through the high wooden doors. The air inside the vast domed lobby is cool, but dry. The floor is made of big blocks of stone and the walls are lined with large gold-framed portraits of unsmiling old men in black judicial robes. A guard in a green uniform sits with his feet up on a scratched gray desk. He looks up from his newspaper and jerks his head, motioning you through a metal detector.

Beep! Beep! Beep! The detector goes berserk. Feel a flash of fear, as if it's not a metal detector at all, but a kids-who-are-ditching-school alarm.

The guard rolls his eyes and heaves himself up from behind his desk. "Take off the backpack," he orders. "Put it on the table."

Do as you're told and step through the metal detector again. No beeps this time. Meanwhile, the guard pokes around inside your backpack, then slides it toward you. "Must have been the zippers. Go on."

You're eager to get as far from this guy as possible. Look down a long wide corridor with high ceilings and many wooden doors, all of them closed. Reluctantly turn back to the guard.

"Could you tell me where I'd find the courtroom where Lawrence Hunter is on trial?"

"Criminal or civil?"

"Uh, criminal, I guess."

"Second floor. Check the dockets on the doors."

Each door on the second floor has a white sheet of paper hanging on it. Outside the door marked "Hon. Judith Moore" the paper reads:

Case #	Defendant name	Charge
3H007-204	Hunter, Lawrence	Burg2
		B&E1
		Trsps1

Go in. Against the far wall a blond woman wearing serious glasses and a black robe sits at a tall desk and faces everyone. This is the Honorable Judith Moore. A red-haired man in a blue suit stands before her, speaking. It's Shragdozer. Judge Moore's head is tilted down as if she's reading and listening at the same time. Two bored-looking court officers with white shirts and gun belts stand with their arms crossed. A well-dressed older couple with gray hair sits in the public gallery. Something tells you they're either the Reynoldses or the Chandlers.

Your parents aren't there. Recall them saying something about a really important teleconference with the Chinese Minister of Communications that day. Otherwise you'd like to believe they'd be in the seats, too.

Uncle Lawrence is sitting alone at a table labeled "Defendant." Writing on a pad of yellow paper. Go down the aisle and into the row of seats behind him. Meanwhile, Shragdozer makes his point with the judge: "Your Honor, my client, Mr. Hunter, has returned all the property he took. He has stated that he is sorry for what he did. He has spoken of his desire to change his ways and find an honest line of work. I ask that the court show mercy and understanding by granting him a suspended sentence."

The well-dressed couple in the gallery mutter to each other and shake their heads in disapproval. Shragdozer straightens his blue suit and returns to the defendant's table. Uncle Lawrence slides the yellow pad in front of him. Judge Moore gazes at a computer screen in the corner of her desk.

"Lawrence." Try to speak quietly, but it still comes out too loud.

Your uncle, and just about everyone else in the court-room, twists around. Even Judge Moore looks up. If only you had a video camera to catch all the expressions that cross Uncle Lawrence's face. From astonishment, to confusion, and finally a big smile.

Give him a thumbs-up. He wrinkles his nose, as if to say it's going to take a lot more than that to get him out of this mess.

"The court will adjourn for fifteen minutes," Judge Moore announces. "I will see counsel in my chambers."

She rises, as does Shragdozer and a man in a black suit from the prosecutor's table. The white-shirted guards escort Uncle Lawrence toward a door to the right of the judge's bench that will take him out of the court-room. Just before he goes through, he turns and winks at you.

The fifteen minutes stretch to twenty and then twenty-five. Stay huddled and shivering in your seat, your damp, cold clothes clinging to your skin, preventing you from getting warm. Legs pressed together. Hugging yourself in a feeble attempt to find some comfort. Don't dare move, or even look around, for fear that someone will notice that you don't belong there on a school day.

The men in suits and Judge Moore return and take their seats again. The white-shirted court officers escort Uncle Lawrence back into the courtroom. He purses his lips and gives you a grim look. You can't tell if it's his way of saying things look really bad, or that you shouldn't have come all this way to see him. But you had to come. If your uncle gets sent away, he can go knowing someone cares. And that his decision to come back wasn't a mistake.

Then a door creaks at the back of the courtroom. And Dr. Rodriguez steps in.

Emotion Fest

you can't take your eyes off her as she comes down the aisle and slides into your row. A beige raincoat is folded over her arm and her bright red umbrella drips rainwater. She smiles warmly and doesn't seem bothered that you're there. In fact, it's you who whispers, "What are you doing here?"

At the sound of your voice, Uncle Lawrence twists around again. It's like a bomb going off when he sees her. But through the bulging eyes and half-open mouth, you can see that he's glad she's there. Really glad.

"Ahem!" Judge Moore clears her throat. "Mr. Hunter?"

Your uncle quickly swivels around and rises to his feet. "Yes, Your Honor?"

"You have expressed regret over these crimes and voiced your desire to begin a new and honest life," the judge says. "That's all very fine and good. There's just one point I'm not quite clear on. Would you please explain to the court *why* it should believe you?"

Uncle Lawrence glances at Shragdozer, who nods back as if to say, *This is your shot, make the best of it.*

"Your Honor," Uncle Lawrence begins, "one thing people don't realize about being a thief is that it's a very, very lonely way to live. It's not like you can tell people what you do for a living. You can't make friends. And if you don't want to get caught, you have to keep moving all the time."

The black-suited lawyer at the prosecution table jerks his head up. Murmurs race through the gallery. At first you don't understand what's going on. Then Shragdozer jumps to his feet.

"Excuse me, Your Honor!" he blurts. "I'm sure my client is speaking in generalizations. He doesn't mean to imply that he speaks from personal experience."

Judge Moore leans forward, raising her chin; her eyes are squarely on Uncle Lawrence. "Just what *do* you mean, Mr. Hunter?"

The courtroom goes silent.

"I mean exactly what I said," your uncle replies. "I lived that way for many years. Always alone. Always moving. It wasn't easy, but the truth is, I didn't think there was any other way to get along."

"Oh, Lord!" Shragdozer groans and buries his face in his hands. Mr. Black Suit at the prosecution table smiles and begins scribbling on his own yellow pad. The crowd murmurs again, stunned that Uncle Lawrence would admit that he's been a thief for a long time. The well-dressed older couple smiles with pleasure.

"And what caused your sudden change of heart?" Judge Moore asks, now clearly interested.

Uncle Lawrence turns to Dr. Rodriguez and you. "I met two people who helped me see that I don't have to live that way. I don't have to be alone. And I don't have to be a thief. That's why I went back to Deep Meadow, Your Honor. Because I realized I didn't want to leave these people."

You've been watching your uncle so closely that you haven't realized that nearly everyone else in the room is staring at you. They're staring because tears are pouring out of your eyes, tickling your nose and feeling hot on your cheeks. Next to you Dr. Rodriguez sniffs and fumbles in her bag for a tissue.

Look up at the judge's bench and see that the Honorable Judith Moore is taking in this whole scene: Uncle Lawrence, Dr. Rodriguez and you in one great big emotion fest.

She clears her throat. "Counsel, please approach the bench."

Promises

Shragdozer and Mr. Black Suit go up and huddle with Judge Moore. They speak in hushed tones. Uncle Lawrence sits down in front of you and Dr. Rodriguez.

"Thanks for coming," he whispers.

"No sweat," you answer, rubbing the last of the tears out of your eyes.

Next to you, Dr. Rodriguez blows her nose and tries to give him a hopeful look. The moment is jarred by abrupt angry tones from the two lawyers speaking to Judge Moore. You catch snippets of what they're saying.

Black Suit: "He just admitted on the record that he's a career criminal."

Shragdozer: "But he says he's changed."

Black Suit: "Did you think he'd say that he intends to *continue* being a thief?"

Shragdozer: "I happen to believe him."

Black Suit: "You also happen to be defending him. Your Honor, this is a complete no-brainer. This guy isn't going to change. The only way to stop him from stealing is to put him in jail and leave him there."

Uncle Lawrence props his chin on his fist. "Looks like I'm going to have plenty of time to decide what I'll do next."

Something makes you suspect he's really asking a question. One you're glad to answer.

"I'll still be here when you decide," you tell him.

"Promise?" he asks.

"On my Swiss Army knife."

Uncle Lawrence grins, then turns his gaze to Dr. Rodriguez. You realize that he's asking her the same question, only this time without words.

"Yes," she whispers. "I promise, too."

A Deal

No sentence will come today. The Honorable Judith Moore wants time to think. The court officers escort Uncle Lawrence through the exit near the judge's bench. As the door swings closed, you catch a glimpse of your uncle placing his hands behind his back, and the glint of steel handcuffs. Feel Dr. Rodriguez's hand on your arm. Time to go. Outside the courthouse, the rain has slowed to a heavy mist. The two of you go down the wet steps, passing through a foggy dreamscape. It does feel like a dream. The lawyers arguing. The glint of those handcuffs. Hard to believe that your uncle's fate is no longer his to decide. He is a prisoner. A stranger in a black judicial robe will decide how he will spend a big chunk of the future.

"We better get you back to school," Dr. Rodriguez says as you both step around the puddles in the parking lot.

"Probably too late for that," you answer.

Her car is a black Acura, as clean and neat as the day it arrived from the factory. Get in. Start to shiver again. You're thankful when she cranks up the heat.

"What are you going to tell your mom?" she asks as she drives.

Check your watch. "School just ended. If we get back soon enough, she'll think I caught the bus home."

"Good."

"Except I've probably been marked absent from all my afternoon classes," you realize out loud.

"Is that something a note from your psychologist could take care of?"

"Definitely worth a try."

Grin at each other. Dr. Rodriguez looks back at the road. "I'm afraid I have some bad news, Martin. Given what's happened, I don't think it's right for us to continue seeing each other."

That catches you off guard, but doesn't bother you as much as you might have expected. Truth is, you never quite understood why you were seeing her in the first place. But your parents insisted and it was easier to go than to fight with them.

"I'll speak to your parents about it," she continues. "To be honest, I'm not sure you really need to see anyone. You've always struck me as a levelheaded young man who's coped reasonably well in a stressful situation."

"But I like you," you protest.

"And I like you, Martin. Just because I won't be treating you doesn't mean we can't be friends."

"Oh, right," you scoff. "Like we'll hang out together."

"Lawrence got pretty good at Double Tap, didn't he?"

"So?"

"I'm better."

What!? "No way."

"Very much way."

"You didn't even know what Double Tap was."

"I was curious, so he showed me. We started playing. It's fun."

She's telling the truth. It explains how Uncle Lawrence improved between the times you played him.

"And I'd like to try air hockey, too," she adds.

You can't help smiling. "That's a deal."

The Idiot's Guide

She drops you off at the foot of your driveway. Wet pebbles make a scratchy, squeaky sound under your shoes. Dreamscape mist wafts through the bare, dark tree trunks and branches.

"Martin?" your mom calls from the kitchen after you let yourself in. "Can you explain a sacrifice fly to me?"

She's sitting at the kitchen table wearing a navy blue sweatshirt and jeans and reading a big black-and-yellow book called *The Idiot's Guide to Coaching Baseball.* Her lips part when she sees you. "You're all wet."

"I'll change clothes." Point at the book. "You serious?"

"You asked if one of us would coach, remember?"

"Sure, but—"

"But what?"

"You really don't have to, Mom."

"You don't want me to?"

"I do, Mom. It's just . . . I don't know. You being around and everything. I have to get used to it."

The phone rings. You answer.

"Martin?" It takes a moment before you realize it's Wendell. You've never heard his voice on the phone before. "How'd it go with your uncle?"

Almost answer, then realize that your mom's there. "I'll have to tell you later."

"Can't talk now?"

"Right."

"So, uh, want to do something?"

It's Friday. You could do something if you wanted to. "Like what?"

"I don't know. Hang out at the mall?"

"Hold on." Ask Mom, "Think you could drop a friend and me at the mall?"

Mom's eyes light up. Like she's been waiting her whole life for this. "Of course."

Back to the phone. "Wendell, you ever play Double Tap?"

"That video game?"

"Yeah."

"A couple of times. You want to play?"

"Thinkin' about it."

"Cool."

Get directions to the farm and tell him you'll be over in half an hour. That'll give you time to change into dry clothes and stop at the store for a fresh supply of Altoids. Hang up and start out of the kitchen.

"Martin?" Mom calls.

"Yeah?"

"Elka's leaving."

"When?"

"Tomorrow. We're having a little going-away party for her tonight, okay?"

"Wouldn't miss it."

The mall with Wendell is fun. You both play about an hour of Double Tap and then mess around in the music store, sampling stuff. Best of all, Wendell brings his own canister of mouth spray.

Later you have the party for Elka. Mom serves a roast chicken dinner she cooked herself. By the time she brings out the homemade chocolate cake, your father is glancing at his watch. His cell phone rings and he reaches into his pocket.

"Let it go," Mom says.

"But it's business."

Mom arches an eyebrow. Your father lets the phone ring. Over tea and cake Mom says, "Elka, I feel we owe you an apology for Lawrence."

"Why?" Elka asks.

Your parents shoot uncertain glances at each other. "Well, for what he turned out to be."

"He was great," Elka replies. "He taught me to play air hockey and keep my eye on the puck. He helped in the kitchen, and he helped with Martin when I had trouble with the car. I'm sorry for what happened, but you don't have to apologize." She reaches toward you and rubs your head. "And this one helped, too. I'll miss you, Martin."

"I'll miss you, Elka."

Your parents are speechless.

Broken Glass

A warm Saturday afternoon in early summer. The bright sun heats your head and shoulders. The air smells like fresh hay and wildflowers. Uncle Lawrence, Dr. Rodriguez and you sit at a picnic table made of hard plastic. It was once red, but the sun has bleached it to light pink. The plastic is hot to the touch, but under your bare arms it feels good. Your uncle is wearing a bright orange jumpsuit. All around you at other faded red picnic tables, men in orange jumpsuits sit with visitors. All the picnic tables are inside a grassy area surrounded by a triple set of chain-link fences topped with glinting coils of razor wire. Prison guards wearing sunglasses and dark green uniforms stroll among the tables and watch from towers.

You and Dr. Rodriguez drove for nearly five hours before entering the gates of Bentonville State Prison. Your parents came here twice during the spring, but this is your first visit.

Uncle Lawrence's skin is pale. It was a rainy spring and you have the feeling he didn't get out much. The Honorable Judith Moore sentenced him to three to five years here in Bentonville. With good behavior he may be out in twenty-two months.

"What do you do all day?" you ask.

"Read, exercise, wonder what I'll do when I get out of this place," he answers.

"Any ideas?" you ask.

"I'd like to work for a security company," he says.

"You mean, like a company that helps people protect themselves against burglars?"

"Exactly. Who better to show them the tricks of the trade than me?"

He has a good point.

"Any other plans?" Dr. Rodriguez asks.

Uncle Lawrence chuckles, then turns to you. "Doc, mind taking a stroll?"

"No sweat." Get up and go over to look at the triple row of fences. A big white sign with a red lightning bolt warns you that the middle fence is electrified. The fences don't end at the ground like normal ones do. They go down into it, as if to stop anyone from tunneling out.

Back at the picnic table Uncle Lawrence and Dr. Rodriguez are leaning close to each other, whispering and holding hands.

Gross. But to be expected.

Walk along the fences until a glint of bright light from the other side catches your attention. Curious as always, you follow the glimmering light and come across a small junk heap. Through the fences you can see some car tires, a sink, some damaged wooden chairs, the metal frame of a bed and a broken mirror, which is the source of the light.

Squint your eyes and the light from the mirror becomes a kaleidoscope of changing colors. Things sure have changed in your life. You're taller, and thinner, and a clearly visible amount of dark hair has finally sprouted above your upper lip. Wendell has become a friend. You often hang with him after school and join in pickup basketball games. Neither of you is close to the best, but you're sometimes needed just to fill out a team. As a result, you're getting better. In fact, you recently challenged Dad to some one-on-one on the court at your house.

And you creamed him.

So now, of course, he wants a rematch.

This summer you'll be old enough to caddie at the club. On slow days you'll get to play. You've already ridden your bike over to the driving range a few times to practice your drives. Practicing isn't as bad as you thought, and your drives are definitely getting straighter. It will take longer to beat Dad in golf, but now that you can beat him in basketball, you're motivated.

He's not such a bad guy, your dad. He always wanted

the right things for you; he just chose the wrong way to show it. The other day you actually got him to leave work early and play miniature golf over at Buzzy's Mini-golf on Route 12. Later, over soft vanilla ice cream cones, you told him what you'd told Uncle Lawrence the morning you'd driven to the airport: that you'd figured out that you didn't have to *be* the best, you just had to *try* your hardest.

And Dad admitted that he knew that was true, but that sometimes he forgot. Then he asked you to keep reminding him.

Now you glance again at the broken mirror lying in the junk heap.

That's the thing about glass.

Sometimes it is more beautiful when it's broken.

But most of the time it's not.

Todd Strasser has written more than one hundred books for young readers, including the international best-seller *Give a Boy a Gun*, *Close Call*, and *Kidnap Kids*. He is the author of the popular "Help! I'm Trapped in . . ." series, including *Help! I'm Trapped in My Teacher's Body* and *Help! I'm Trapped in Obedience School*, as well as *Don't Get Caught in the Girl's Locker Room* and *Hey, Dad, Get a Life!* He frequently speaks at schools about the craft of writing and conducts writing workshops for young people. Todd Strasser lives in a suburb of New York City.